NEW ALLEYS FOR NOTHING MEN

Noir Stories

MICHAEL POOL

NEW ALLEYS FOR NOTHING MEN

Short Stack Books is a registered US trademark.

The following stories have been previously published and some have been extensively revised. "Waylon, On Rerun" in *Thuglit Issue 18*; "Tote the Note" in *All Due Respect Issue 4*; "An Art Show Mating Call" in *Urban Graffiti (online)*; "Two Feet Deep" in *Heater Magazine Vol. 3 No. 9*; "Franklin and the Finger" in *Out of the Gutter's Flash Fiction Offensive (online)*; "Life of a Salesman" in *That Other Paper (online)*.

Cover designed by Michael Pool
Formatting by Rik Hall – Wild Seas Formatting
(http://www.wildseasformatting.com)

ISBN 978-0-9968552-1-1

First Edition revised

ACKNOWLEDGEMENTS

Special thanks for all the love and support from the crime fiction community, my mother Kathy Mitchell, my brother Mark Pool, and my stepfather George Mitchell. And also to Ralph Martin, gone but never forgotten.

Shout out to the Master Assassins: Nathan Beauchamp, Chris Barili, Jeff Bowles, Austin Rodgers, and Anna Schuett. Thanks to Mark Todd, Michaela Roessner Herman, and Russell Davis for all the guidance. Thanks to all the publications who published stories that appear in this collection, ya'll are awesome human beings.

There are too many more people to mention, though please know you're all appreciated. Cheers!

"I took up writing to escape the drudgery of that every day cubicle kind of a war." – Walter Mosley

Contents

WAYLON, ON RERUN

WAYLON HAD ALREADY LOADED up the microwave, the DVD player, a desktop computer and half the food in the fridge when the aging, mentally challenged man showed up at the chain link fence that lined the back alley behind the house.

"Hello," the man said, squinting against the sun as Waylon moved past him to the back of his pumpkin-colored van. "This is Mr. Collins' house?"

Waylon nodded, even though he had no idea whose house it was. He tried to figure whether or not the retarded grey-haired man he recognized from the thrift store a few blocks over would be able to identify him later. Maybe. But the goddamn television was heavy, and he couldn't move it by himself. The pock-skinned man stared off down the alley like a child might.

"What's your name there, partner?" Waylon asked.

The man did an about-face like Waylon had learned in ROTC back in high school, before he discovered heroin out on the rodeo circuit.

"Oh. I'm Bernie. Are you here helping Mr. Collins too?"

"You bet."

Wanna know what?" Bernie asked.

"What's that, bub?"

"You should get a mohawk, shawty." Bernie pointed at Waylon's shaggy hair and grinned, revealing a mouth with half the teeth missing.

Waylon sighed. Bernie had said the same thing when Waylon came through his line at the thrift store a few weeks back, the day after he got out of the klink this last time. It had taken almost ten minutes for Bernie to ring him up. Enough time to tell the same joke four times. One of the volunteers at the store must have taught Bernie to use the term "shawty," without telling him what it meant.

"You think so?" Waylon said, keeping his voice friendly.

"Aww, I'm just jokin'," Bernie said, then grinned again.

"What can I say, Bernie? You got me. Anyway, my name's Charlie Daniels, and Mr. Collins told me to ask for your help."

"Mr. Collins says I'm a good helper."

"Well it's my lucky day then, Bernie, because I could use a strong fella like you to help move his television set into the van here."

"Because Mr. Collins don't want to watch no more?" Bernie asked.

"Well—ah—not exactly. I wanna borrow it from him, but I can't carry it by myself."

"But how will he watch his shows? I watch lots of shows."

Waylon forced a smile. "I guess he'll have to manage. Anyhow, Could you come inside and give me a hand?"

"Sure thing, shawty."

"You are a good helper, Bernie, Mr. Collins is right."

"Missus Collins says God made me to be a helper."

"She must be real proud of you, then. Follow me, bubba." Waylon walked through the garage into the kitchen, which he'd torn apart looking for stashed money, then into the living room. Bernie stayed right on his heels.

"The television is right over —"

"*Ding-dong the witch is dead! Ding-dong the witch is dead! Ding-dong!*" Bernie called out, jumping up and down and pointing at something over Waylon's left shoulder. Waylon followed Bernie's eyes to a set of commemorative plates for *The Wizard of Oz* arranged on a built-in bookshelf. One of them had the Wicked Witch of the West's green face painted on it. Bernie's eyes swelled to the size of jawbreakers as he pointed at the plate and shuffled his hips like he needed to pee.

"It's just a plate, Bernie, calm down," Waylon said.

Bernie's face turned bright red. "*Ding dong,*" he said again, with less conviction this time. "I don't like the witch. She sets the Scarecrow on fire. Then shawty comes and throws the bucket of water all over The Witch, and she melts like ice cream. I'm glad she melted."

"Well I'm glad too, Bernie." Waylon walked over

3

to the plate and set it flat, so that the face was no longer visible. One of the other plates in the set gave him an idea. "I'll tell you what. You like the Scarecrow?" Waylon asked.

"Yeah. I like for him to dance," Bernie said.

"Well look at this." Waylon reached up to the top shelf, took the plate with the Scarecrow caught midway through some sort of jig painted on it down and showed it to Bernie. "Mr. Collins has a plate with the Scarecrow on it too. He said if you help me move the television out, it's yours."

"Really?" Bernie asked, the Wicked Witch seeming gone from his mind now. "I can take it home?"

"You can take it home, eat dinner off of it, whatever you want."

"I can't use that for eating, but I could just look at it I guess." The first traces of a grin formed on Bernie's face.

"Hell Bernie, you can give it a mohawk if that's what you want," Waylon said. "But for now, let's just get the television moved. I'm running a little late."

"But don't forget to let me have the plate after," Bernie said, ignoring Waylon's request.

"I won't forget, I promise," Waylon assured him. "Deal? Now if you'll just get the other side of this television ... there you go, and now on a count of three let's lift it together and carry it out. Ready? One— two—three."

They lifted the television together. Waylon swung around so that he would be the one moving backwards as they took the television up the two steps into the kitchen toward the back door.

They made it up the steps and were halfway to

the back door when Bernie dropped his end without warning, brought his wrists up to his armpits like wings and yelled *"Cockadoodledoo!"* while flapping his bent elbows up and down like a rooster. Waylon yelped and dropped his end too. The set landed on Waylon's left foot, and he knew without looking that both the Television set and his foot were broken. He gasped as a throbbing pain shot up his leg to his spine.

"Goddammit Bernie," he yelled, hopping on his good foot now. "Goddammit, goddammit. You stupid son of a bitch. I think you broke my fucking foot. You definitely broke the damn television!"

Bernie looked horrified, but kept glancing beyond Waylon at the ceramic rooster on top of the fridge, almost reaching up as if to flap his wings more, then stopping and sinking back into the horrified look again. His top lip quivered and his eyes welled up. Waylon wished right away he'd not let his temper go like that.

"I'm … I'm sorry," Bernie mumbled, "I didn't mean to drop the television. I'm so stupid." He repeated the last part again and then slapped himself across the face, hard. Then again. He threw himself to the ground next to the cratered television set and began banging his head against the linoleum floor. He'd already managed to leave a series of welts and splits in his forehead, as well as deep hand marks on his cheeks, before Waylon could shimmy over to try and make him stop.

"*Stupid, Stupid, Stupid,*" Bernie said, "I don't know why I'm so stupid."

"Hey, just take it easy," Waylon said, trying to sound authoritative as he attempted to restrain Bernie's hands. Bernie was much stronger than he looked. He ripped his hands away and continued going to town on himself, until finally Waylon said "Fuck it" and bowled him over flat on his back. He sat on Bernie's chest like a horse. "Relax, Bernie. RELAX," he said, pinning Bernie's arms to the floor.

Bernie squirmed and struggled to no avail. He didn't seem to want or be able to calm down. Waylon didn't want to hit him, but he couldn't afford to waste much more time there. he needed to get Bernie under control, collect anything left of remaining value, and get out. Bernie slobbered and moaned, yanked at his arms more like he wanted to hit himself again. Waylon held him down as best he could, not sure what else to do.

"What in God's name are you two doing in my house?" a gruff voice said behind Waylon. "My God — Bernie, is that you?"

"Hello Mr. Collins," Bernie replied, shifting gears in an instant, no longer struggling under Waylon's grip now. "I came to help after church, like you said. I could give you a mohawk now if you want? Just jokin!"

"So you did, and so I see," the old man said, his voice barely able to hide the rage on his face, but maybe attempting to do so for Bernie's sake. "Mister," he added, "I don't know who you are or why you're in my house, but you'd best get off Bernie before Mora comes in and —"

"Before I come in and what?" a woman with a daisy-topped straw hat said from over the old man's shoulder. She shrieked when she noticed Waylon sitting on Bernie. "Bernie," she said, her startled eyes taking in the scene, the busted television, emptied cabinets, everything really. "What are you doing to my sweet, sweet Bernie?"

Waylon had never felt so low in his life. He released Bernie's arms and started to stand up. Though her husband looked to be in some sort of shock, Mora didn't seem have the same problem.

"You were abusing my Bernie," she screamed at Waylon. "How could you? He's *special*. What kind of monster are you?" she added, her voice shaking now.

"Now just hold up, ma'am," Waylon tried to explain as he moved to stand up. "He was hitting hisself and —" Before Waylon could finish, the woman snatched the ceramic rooster from the top of the fridge and swung it with both hands like a sledgehammer. The rooster shattered against the side of Waylon's face and he crumbled to the ground, unconscious.

* * *

Waylon came to with a splitting headache and blood running down his face. He tried to reach up and massage his temples only to discover that his hands were bound behind his back instead. He remembered where he was then. His eyes wouldn't focus for a moment. When they finally did focus, he was staring straight into the chrome barrel of a .357 lawman pistol.

"You just stay still and take it easy there mister," said Mr. Collins, who Waylon recognized now as the manager of the thrift store where he'd first seen Bernie.

"I don't think I could move if I tried," Waylon replied.

"That's good," Collins said, "You probably wouldn't live long enough to try anything else if you did. The police are on their way. In the meantime, maybe you'd like to explain how you came to find yourself abusing a poor, mentally-handicapped man like Bernie in our home?"

"I don't guess there's much to say, then," Waylon replied.

Collins cocked the hammer on the pistol and poked Waylon in the forehead with the barrel's tip. "I'm of the mind there's plenty to say," he said.

Waylon sighed and let his shoulders slump. "Okay, I get your drift. What can I say? I was robbing the place when Bernie showed up at the back fence. I knew it was stupid when I done it, but I couldn't carry the television by myself. Goddamn thing's so old I probably couldn't have gotten twenty bucks for it anyway, with all these flat- screens around these days. Fact remains, I needed that twenty. So I got Bernie to help me carry the television out. Except he dropped it. Apparently he's got a thing for roosters and commemorative plates."

Collins released the hammer and let the gun's barrel pan down to the floor. Waylon took a deep breath.

"You some kind of addict, or just an idiot?" Collins asked. "Because those are the only two reasons why I can imagine a man robbing a house in broad daylight on a Sunday. Given that you got Bernie involved, I'm assuming it's probably a combination of the two."

"When you're right, you're right, I reckon," Waylon said, measuring his words. "But I want ya'll to know something. I wasn't hurting Bernie. I might be a thief, but I ain't no bully. My daddy bout whipped me to death way back when I was a kid, and I'd never lay my hands on someone like that. After Bernie dropped your television, he got all worked up and started whipping on hisself. I was trying to stop him when ya'll come in and jacked me up with the rooster." Waylon wanted to rub his head where the rooster had connected.

"I see," Collins said, his face softening a little. "Well, he's been known to do that, unfortunately. I think it's probably pretty frustrating being Bernie, wouldn't you say? I hope you're satisfied with yourself, though. This whole thing's scared the daylights out of him. Mora's back there trying to calm him down now. Not to mention you've destroyed our home to nobody's benefit."

"I get it," Waylon said. "I do. I'm actually surprised you haven't already shot my dumb ass, though I'm thankful for your mercy. I'm sorry about all this, really I am. Truth is, I'm a junkie. It's a hell of a thing, but I just can't keep my country ass off the dope. Even sitting here right now, feeling like the low down piece of shit that I am, part of me's thinking whether or not I'll be able to score a hit in county lockup. The answer is maybe. I know you probably don't want to hear that, but it's the truth."

"There's a certain irony to it, Mr. ... I didn't catch your name?"

"Name's Waylon Tompkins. I'd say pleased to meet you, but I don't want to feed ya'll any more bullshit today."

"Mr. Tompkins," Collins said, as if trying out his name. "Waylon. I understand you more than you think, Waylon Tompkins. As it happens, my son Jacob died from a heroin overdose in this very house. The only way Mora and I managed to survive it was to make it our mission in life to help addicts such as yourself. Addicts, and also some of the mentally handicapped, though anyone observing us right now might say there's not much difference in the two when it comes to decision making."

"Yeah, they might say that, I guess," Waylon said.

"Now let me give you some truth. I'd like to help you, Waylon," Collins said, using his name now as if they were old friends. "The way I see it, a person has to be out of their mind with sickness to trick a mentally disabled man into helping him rob the home of people who would give him the shirts off their backs anyway. The only people around town who provide work, shelter, and stability for a man like Bernie. And also for men like yourself."

Waylon frowned, still wanting to rub his swollen head. "Had I known it, I would've picked someplace else," he said.

"You see, that's just it, Waylon. There is no place else. It's all one big place. That you would victimize anyone anywhere is a sign that something important is broken inside you. I'd like to help you fix it, if you decide you want to try."

"So you're not gonna press charges, then?" Waylon asked, hopeful.

"I didn't say that, Waylon," Collins replied. "Accountability is the currency of civilization. You've accrued a debt to your fellow man, and now you'll have to make things whole with him. But once you get free from that, if you want to, you could come work at the shop and stay at our shelter. So long as you stay clean and work our program."

Waylon started to reply, but someone pounded on the front door and they both looked up instead.

"Looks like your ride's here," Collins said. "Let's get you up and at 'em." Collins kept the gun in his right hand and grasped Waylon's inner bicep with his left. He helped Waylon to his feet. "You just remember what I said, Waylon Tompkins," he said as they moved into the living room. "We run The Lord's Salvation Thrift Store here in town. You pay your debt to society and want to stay clean afterward, then you come see us."

"I might just do that," Waylon said, knowing it was another lie even as the words were escaping his lips. The look on Collins' face said he knew it too.

Collins led him by the arm into the living room just as his wife Mora opened the door to reveal two police officers, each with a hand on his pistol. Both cops glared at Waylon before the bigger one, who had a thick moustache, spoke.

"Get face down on the ground," he said. "NOW."

Waylon complied as best he could with his hands bound, dropped to his knees and then lay face down like the cop instructed. Collins guided him by the arm all the way to the ground, then let go and stepped back.

"We found him in the kitchen," Collins said. "He's got a van back in the alley with some of our stuff in it, too."

The cops stepped up and flanked Waylon on either side. Waylon winced when they each drove a knee into his kidneys. They replaced whatever had been used to bind his hands with a set of handcuffs instead, then yanked him to his feet by the cuffs.

"Shit, man, ouch," Waylon said. "I'm compliant. Ya'll don't have to be so rough about it."

The mustached cop slapped him upside the head. "Stop resisting," he said.

"Easy there, gentlemen," Collins said. "No need

for that. I think he's had enough for today."

Neither of the cops replied, but they didn't hit Waylon again, either. Instead they led him toward the front door.

"Does this mean I don't get the Scarecrow?" Bernie said from behind him. Waylon craned his neck around so that he could just see the edge of Bernie's tear-streaked face poking out the bathroom door.

"That ain't up to me now, bub," Waylon said. "I'm sorry I got you into this mess, though. I get out, I'll bring you a Scarecrow plate, up at your work. Sound okay?" Another lie.

Bernie seemed to be waiting for permission from Collins to speak. The old man nodded his head.

"Okay, shawty," Bernie said, grinning again now. "Sorry about the television. I guess you won't get to watch your shows now either."

Waylon knew they had cable in county lockup but figured this wasn't a good time to bring it up. "I guess not," he said instead.

"You come see us when you get out," Collins said. Waylon nodded as the cops moved him out the front door.

"When you bring the plate I could give you a mohawk," Bernie said.

"I suppose you could, Bernie," Waylon called over his shoulder, thinking how the old woman had already pretty much given him one with the rooster anyway.

"I'm just jokin!" Bernie said. As the officers led Waylon out to the backseat of a cruiser parked at the curb, he couldn't help wondering if it was the truth.

TOTE THE NOTE

KARL JOYCE LET THE travel trailer's flimsy door slam shut behind him as he popped open another Budweiser and lit another smoke. The summer night's air was so muggy that sweat soaked through his undershirt to form a dark puddle on his chest. His hands shook as he drew deep pulls from the cigarette that left the butt soggy, its cherry stretched out into an inch-long ember.

He studied the house just across the driveway, *his* house, built with his own money. The light in his wife's bedroom turned off as he watched, the last one still lit in the house. The house felt far away in spite of being no more than thirty feet from the travel trailer to which his family had recently exiled him.

Karl took another long pull off the Budweiser to drain it, opened the trailer door and tossed it inside on the floor. He let the door slam shut so loud he was certain the lights in the house would come back on. He *wanted* them to come on. This was *his* goddamned house. *His* goddamned property. He'd make as much noise as he pleased, drink as much beer as he pleased, and smoke as much crack cocaine as he damn well felt necessary.

This arrangement would work just fine for him, he told himself. No more listening to his boys fighting about stupid shit all the time. No more Claudia bitching and moaning about his drinking. He was a grown man, and the breadwinner for this goddamned family. To Karl that meant he could do whatever the hell he wanted whether they liked it or not.

Besides, they had no idea what it took to get through his days. Through the irate customers and shit bag clunkers that always needed repairs, not to mention the unbearable stress brought down on him in recent weeks by the IRS auditor, a man named Timothy Sorren, who seemed to want nothing more than to ruin Karl's life.

Sorren had shown up unannounced a few weeks earlier, telling him that the United States Government had found a few discrepancies with his car dealership's tax returns. He'd emphasized those words in his monotone little voice. *A few*. It had made Karl shiver. In reality the last couple years' entire returns had been nothing *but* discrepancies, if that's what you wanted to call them.

Goddamn Sorren with his pointy nose and ratty eyes hidden behind wire-rimmed glasses. His suffocating poise and lack of humor, which made it impossible to warm up to him on any level. Karl decided within the first hour that he'd crack the man's goddamn skull open if he ever got the chance to get away with it.

Karl thought again now about all the cash payments he'd erased from the dealership's system and pocketed, what must have been tens of thousands of dollars. He felt sure he hadn't spent *all* of it on booze, cocaine and pills, that at least some of it must have been used for the good of his family. But somehow it had been spent and he couldn't un-spend it even if he wanted to.

Most recently he'd been forced to start repossessing cars in spite of their owners' on-time payments, hoping to make the money back fast enough to cover his tracks. Most of his customers never bothered to ask for receipts to their payments, and all of them paid in cash. When they showed up at the dealership, irate, they lacked proof to verify their accounts were current, which meant that his plan had been working, to a degree, though now he was certain he had at least five people who wanted him dead.

All this craziness would, sooner or later, have to come to light, he realized that now. If not for the beer and pills and cocaine, this audit would have already been the death of him. It still might be, one way or the other. He slammed the entire contents of his beer and crushed the empty can in his fist. In his heart Karl knew that soon enough this house and the thirty acres it sat on would probably be gone. He'd be lucky even to be around to see that.

He stepped back into the trailer, tossed the crushed can onto the floor and snagged another Budweiser from the small refrigerator. He popped it open as the trailer door slammed shut again. He found the little glass pipe where he'd left it, next to the loveseat, which had been brand new only months ago but was now pocked full of burn holes from stray cigarette ashes and discarded bits of sizzling Chore Boy.

He took the package of Chore Boy from the table at the center of the trailer and pinched a little sliver off with a nail clipper.

He stuffed the chunk into the pipe, where the last piece had deteriorated to almost nothing. He picked up the tiny plastic baggy sitting next to the Chore Boy and took out one of the opaque rocks, this one the size of a small piece of gravel. He plugged the pipe with it.

Karl lit the rock and sucked through the pipe. The tip heated up so hot that he winced and pulled his seared lips away from it. He choked for a second or two as he held it in, then blew the thick, metallic smoke out in a cloud that filled the trailer as his heart rate spiked like he'd been struck by lightning. His vision blurred and vibrated. A heat wave pounded through his veins, the rush from the cocaine.

He let out a howl that must have been loud, but the freight train ringing in his ears drowned it out. He tried to focus his eyes on the window above the camper's sink. When they wouldn't focus he picked up his fresh beer and hurled it at the window. The glass fractured into a web but didn't shatter.

He reached for the boom box on the counter's volume knob, cranked it up loud. "Bad Moon," one of his favorite songs, blared from the speakers. He managed to tremble another cigarette from the pack on the table and light it, took a drag and placed it onto the edge of the ashtray, where it sat smoking.

Karl swayed as he stepped to the refrigerator and pulled out another Budweiser. His fingers shook so bad that he had to struggle with the can's tab before he finally tore it open. He paced back and forth through the trailer taking huge slugs of the beer and trying to reestablish his grip on reality, or whatever he existed in these days.

Someone started hammering on the trailer's door, which helped him find the reality he was reaching for in an instant. Was it the police? Or worse, fucking Sorren? Sweat drops cascaded off his forehead into the beer in his hand. He threw a blanket over the table to cover the pipe, his cigarette still smoking there in the ashtray.

"Karl, what in God's name is going on in there?" his wife Claudia yelled from outside the trailer door. "Are you trying to keep us up all night? I'm sure the Mitchums can hear that crazy music in their bedroom a half mile from here."

"Go away Claudia," Karl stammered, relieved that it wasn't Sorren, which made no sense anyway. "Now." He stepped over and flipped the lock up on the door a split second before she tugged on the handle to open it.

"Open this door, Karl. What is that *smell?*"

"Go fuck yourself, Claudia" he called out. "You wanted me out of the house, you got it. But this is my goddamned trailer. Hell, it's my goddamned land. I'll do as I please out here."

"Karl," Claudia said, softer now. "Karl, please. The boys are awake too. Nobody could sleep through all this noise. Don't you care about our boys? Is this how you want them to see you, to *remember* you, drinking and drugging yourself to death not a hundred feet from where they sleep?"

Karl's stomach sank at the mention of his boys, Cody and John. They were good boys, and they deserved better. But *he* deserved better too. Nobody understood the load he bore. None of them appreciated the things he endured for them each day.

His thoughts shifted to a summer years ago when he'd coached their little league baseball team. He could still picture the look of admiration and respect for him in their eyes back then. He doubted he'd be seeing that look again anytime soon.

"You tell them to get back to sleep before I give them something to stay awake over. Matter of fact, you'd best get your ass inside too."

He stood there by the door for another moment waiting for her to speak again, but she didn't. The music was so loud he couldn't tell if she still stood outside. He had to work up the guts to look through the shattered window. When he finally did he saw his wife's silhouette disappearing into the back door of the house.

Karl opened the cabinet above the sink and took out a bottle of Jack Daniels. He fumbled with the top, then took a big draw from the bottle. He replaced the top and put the bottle back on the shelf. The bitter whisky burned in his throat as he swallowed.

At some point, "Bad Moon" had ended and been replaced by The Spencer Davis Group's "Gimme Some Lovin." He'd just calmed down enough to notice the music when someone started banging on the door again.

"Claudia, I told you to *fuck* off," he called out. "Don't make me come—"

His older son Cody's voice cut in, deep for a boy of 17. "You son of a bitch!" Cody yelled, his voice hoarse. "How dare you threaten my mother? We're trying to go to sleep but you're making so much fucking noise it's impossible."

Rage swelled up in Karl's chest. He slammed his beer and spiked the can on the floor. He'd never tolerated back talk from his boys, just as his father had beaten the same kind of insolence out of him.

Karl flipped the lock open and front-kicked the door without unlatching it. The door swung open and caught Cody on the shoulder. He staggered backwards off the first step and into the dirt, wincing. Karl exploded out of the doorway ready to trounce his son.

He felt the ground disintegrate beneath his feet, realized too late he'd forgotten about the steps down. For half a second his arms rolled down the windows in mid-air before he tipped forward and landed hard on his chest.

Cody erupted into laughter. "Oh how the mighty have fallen," he called out, still holding his shoulder where the door had hit him.

Karl sat up slow, dazed. He wiped the dirt off his face with the back of his arm. A trickle of blood ran down his forehead. At the sight of his own blood Karl jumped to his feet, hell-bend on stomping the piss out of his mouthy son. Though Cody was no longer as little as he used to be, Karl still outweighed him by thirty or forty pounds, even if most of that was beer belly.

Cody backed away with his hands up. Karl lunged at him with an overhand right intended to knock the boy's head off his shoulders. Cody circled out and hit him with a stiff jab that left Karl's eye's watering. He should never have taught the boy how to box.

Karl pivoted and charged with a barrage of punches. They slammed into each other and clinched, each scrambling to toss the other to the ground and pummel him. For a moment Karl landed on top, but his balance went bad and Cody rolled him over. As Cody reared back to slam his fist into Karl's face. Karl reached up and dug his nails into the boy's cheeks until Cody squealed and rolled away from him.

Somewhere in the commotion Claudia had appeared. As Karl rolled on top to go in for the kill, she screamed something he couldn't understand above the music. He understood much better when she gripped two hands full of his hair and yanked him backwards. Karl yelped and swung the back of his hand blindly toward his wife. His wrist caught her in the throat and sent her tumbling backwards into the dirt. He didn't have time to turn and look at her before Cody jumped on him again.

Cody slammed a hook into his head that rolled him onto his back in the dirt. He sat up on Karl's chest and slammed two or three good punches into his face that bounced his head off the ground. Just as Karl prepared himself for unconsciousness, Claudia let out a loud shriek.

"FIRE!" she screamed.

Cody drew back and swiveled his head toward the smoke pouring out of the trailer. Karl grabbed him by the throat and tossed him to the side. As Karl rolled on top again his gaze shifted to the smoking trailer. He froze for a second, too confused to keep fighting. Then he remembered that he'd forgotten to put it out in his haste to cover the pipe with the blanket.

He scrambled to his feet and ripped open the dented trailer door. The latch hung loose from where he'd kicked the door before. The table and the thin blue curtains from the window above it were covered in flames. He started to step inside, wanting to somehow put it out. The fire's heat hit him so hard that he staggered backwards and fell down the stairs again. He slammed into the dirt and onto his head with a hollow thud. Everything sank into darkness.

* * *

When Karl came to again, sirens and flashing red lights surrounded him. He thought he must be having a nightmare. As his vision came into focus he realized the flashing lights were from a fire truck and an ambulance. A paramedic hovered above him attempting to shine a light into his eyes. Karl squinted against the light as his vision blurred out again.

"Sir, you've had an accident. Please don't move," the paramedic said.

Karl ignored the man's instructions and swatted his pen-shaped light away. He sat up on his haunches and shook his head out. The trailer was consumed in flames now. Two firefighters flanked it with a hose, attempting to form a line between the raging fire and the house. Some deranged and unintelligible song still blared from within the burning trailer. A gust of wind fanned the flames and in an instant the oak tree Claudia had planted adjacent to the house on the day they moved in caught fire.

Karl's swallowed hard thinking that the house might catch fire He'd built the damn thing himself, not with his hands, but with his time, day in and day out, for *years*. He'd built this family, this life and everything in it upon his suffering.

He'd worked for it day after day in that goddamned prison of a car dealership, built the lot up one car at a time until he had a floor plan of a hundred cars on the average day. *We Tote the Note (Nosotros Financiamos),* the sign that towered above his lot proclaimed, letting potential Hispanic customers know that the dealership would finance them directly, no bank or credit check required. He'd grown tired of carrying that burden after so many years.

Claudia and Cody sat about ten feet away wrapped in emergency blankets. His youngest son John knelt next to them, visibly terrified.

Karl just sat there, too stunned to speak. His life had been on fire for so long it almost felt natural to watch it burn. He wondered who would tote the note for this deal, and shivered as much from the drugs as from the realization that he couldn't imagine a scenario where it could ever be anyone but himself.

TWO FEET DEEP

HARMAN DROVE INTO TOWN through sheets of falling snow, blood still seeping from his belly, the night outside a winter tomb waiting to swallow him. The highway's yellow centerline showed through in patches beneath the packing snowfall. Not much attention from the plow trucks yet for this big of a storm, but that didn't surprise him, the county never seemed to have enough budget to remove all the snow in a given year.

He wanted to light a cigarette, but the old Subaru's windows were frozen shut. He only had one free hand at the moment anyway. His right hand was trapped under his coat holding an old t-shirt over the bloody stab wound in his abdomen.

He needed to get rid of Ray Miller's still-warm body, laid out with a tarp folded over it in the wagon's back end. He hadn't wanted to kill Ray, but the stubborn old man hadn't given him much choice. The man wasn't even supposed to be home, would still be breathing now if he'd just stayed out at bingo like he usually did.

Instead Ray had come home early, Harman had panicked, and he'd killed Ray in the ensuing struggle. Then, even more panicked, he'd drug the body out to his car and fled the scene. Only now did it occur to him he had nowhere to take the body, not to mention that it would probably draw even more attention if Ray just disappeared with his house covered in blood than it would if he were just found murdered.

No way to bury it. The goddamn ground had been frozen for months, would be for months to come. He could drag it somewhere remote and let the wildlife take care of it, but getting anywhere remote would be next to impossible with two feet of snow suffocating the landscape. Even with snowshoes he probably wouldn't make it very far into the woods with a dead body over his shoulders.

He probably should have just let go of Ray's throat once he passed out, but the old man had seen his face, and Harmon didn't want to go back to BVCC. Plus, after the old man stuck him with his pocket knife it had felt like a life or death struggle, kill or be killed. So he had killed, and he would do it again if he had to. No use worrying about that choice now.

Right now he needed to find medical attention, or at least get somewhere safe to wait out the storm so he could think the whole thing through with a clearer head. Everything had happened so fast he hadn't had time to think until this moment. He remembered something his father had once told him: *You burn enough bridges, Harman, you'll find yourself on an island with no way off it one of these days.*

Hard to deny Harman had finally arrived on that island, even if it took the shape of a high mountain town he'd lived in most of his adult life as the town addict. The only way he could see off this island at the moment was to turn to the one thing thicker than the snow boxing him in: his own flesh and blood. He turned onto Main St., certain now of what he had to do to get through the night still breathing.

Sodium lampposts floated by in muted orange blurs outside the wagon's fogged windows. Harmon made a left and plowed a path into one of the alleys just off Main, eased to a stop behind the aging blue A-frame house among otherwise untracked snow. He shut off the engine and eased the old t-shirt that he'd been using as a compress out from under his coat. The sight of his own blood made his knees ache, reminded him again he'd killed a man less than an hour ago.

Harman paused at the back door, afraid to face his only son, who had every right to hate his guts, and pretty well did. Shane had asked him not to come around anymore a year ago, and he'd obliged him the request. If his son hated to see Harman drowning in booze and Oxycontin, making a fool of himself in and out of the three bars around town, it was hard to imagine he'd be thrilled to find his drug-addict father stabbed in the gut and bleeding on the back porch at two a.m.

Harman had no intention of mentioning the body in the car. He wouldn't be able to admit such a thing to Shane anyway, who had acted more like the father between the two of them since he was sixteen. Harman had never acted like much of a father or anything else decent, that he could recall.

He regretted that, though there was nothing he could do about it now. Right now he needed to get patched up and figure a way out of this situation.

So he knocked, trying to keep it down so as not to wake up the neighbors.

It took a few tries before a light came on inside. Harman exhaled when Shane's eyes appeared cupped by hands against the door's window, rather than Fran's. Fran had always hated his guts. Shane leaned away from the window, then back again as if to be sure he'd seen Harman there. Harman nodded. Shane's shape leaned back again, though the deadbolt didn't unlock.

They stood there like that, father and son on opposing sides of glass, just as they'd done when Shane was a teenager and Harman an inmate at BVCC over in Buena Vista. Back then the windows and locks had been there to keep Harman inside. In the current moment he couldn't escape the feeling that they were there to keep him out.

Almost a minute went by, Harmon standing there bleeding on the porch, in pain, really needing some Oxy for that, or at least some sort of something. Shane standing somewhere on the other side of the door, probably cursing whatever fate led him to have such a worthless father.

Harman was about to get in the car and drive away when the lock slid back and the door swung in, revealing Shane in a pair of plaid pajama pants and a Telluride Bluegrass t-shirt.

Shane sighed. "What do you want, Harman?" he said. "It's three-thirty in the morning. I'm supposed to be out the door at five for a plow shift."

"Hey, Shane," Harman began. He wasn't sure

what else to say, so he added, "Yeah, I figured all the snow was keeping you busy. How's Fran?

Another sigh. "Harman, what do you want?"

"Look, Shane, I'm sorry about all that business before. I just lost my mind for a time, is all."

"Lost your—what kind of apology is that? You pawned the .300 mag Granddad left me because you lost your mind? I don't want to hear any of this shit, actually. Have a nice life, Harman." Shane started to shut the door, but Harman wedged his foot in the way.

"Shane, wait. I am sorry. No excuse for that. And you're right. I do need your help. I wouldn't of even come, except I got nowhere else to go."

"Shocking."

"I know that don't come as a surprise. But anyhow, I'm hurt, and I didn't know where else to turn."

"The hospital, maybe?" Shane said. "It's a block over, on Denver."

"I can't go there."

"Cause you're caught up in some kind of criminal bullshit, no doubt." Shane sneered, ran a hand through his hair before he added, "I want no part of it. Take it somewhere else."

"I just thought with your mountain rescue training you might be able to help me patch this up." Harman opened his coat to reveal his bloody clothing below, removed the t-shirt compress in his hand again to expose the wound better.

"Jesus Christ," Shane said. "Are you shot or stabbed?"

"Stabbed. Had a fight with a fella who tried to rip me off," Harman lied. "He got about halfway there."

Shane shook his head. "So call the police, Harman. I really can't help you."

"I can't, Shane," Harman said, trying to make himself look meek now, which never seemed to work anymore. "Every goddamn deputy west of the divide knows me. They find out what was about to get stolen I'm doing five-to-ten for sure."

"You ever consider that five-to-ten might be a good start?"

"Prison's no good for anyone, son. Don't give me that."

"Prison's the place reasonable people send the ones who can't keep their tail out of the trap," Shane said, the frustration evident in his voice now.

Harman started to say something else, but a wave of nausea came on and stopped him. His knees buckled and he had to lean against the doorframe for support.

"Might be that I drop dead here on your porch, I keep losing blood," he said. "I'm not asking you to like me, or forgive me. I'm asking you to *help* me. We're kin. This is your blood leaking out of my belly too."

Shane looked as if he might close the door, hesitated, then took a step back.

"Okay, Harman."

"Okay what?"

Shane exhaled, ran a hand through his hair again. "Okay, I'm going to help you bandage your wound. Then you're out of here. For good. Don't ever come around here again afterwards. EVER. Understood?"

"I get it. Now let me in please, I feel like I might faint." Harman tried to look woozy now, for effect.

Shane let Harmon pass through the back door into a disheveled kitchen. There were dishes stacked in the sink, which was odd for Shane, who had always been anal about organization. Harmon took it all in through shaky vision. Hard to believe he'd managed to strangle a man to death in this state, really.

"Fran don't clean up around here anymore?" Harman asked, realizing only after that he ought to keep his mouth shut, as usual.

Shane bristled and stepped past him. "Fran and I split, Harman," he said as he made his way to the solitary bathroom in the house. He came back into the kitchen with a first aid kit under his arm and a big roll of gauze.

"Split?" Harmon raised his eyebrows.

"Take off your coat."

Harman complied. He eased off his coat to reveal a few additional slash marks along his right arm. "When did that happen?" he asked.

"Really, Harman? We gonna do this now? I'd hate for you to pretend you gave a good goddamn, so why don't we skip the catching up, get you bandaged, and then you can get back to focusing on yourself again full time. Sound good?"

"Come on, Shane," Harmon said, feeling real emotion now, at least. "It was just a question. Believe it or not I care, even if it ain't obvious most of the time."

"She left six months ago. Divorce will be final next week. That's all I'm saying about it. Now can you get your shirt off? Toss it and that bloody compress in the trashcan over there. And try not to get blood all over my damn floor while you do it."

Harman took the shirt he'd been using for a compress over to the trash, saw it was half full and decided against it. Instead, he opened the pantry and found a fresh trash bag, managed to get it open using one arm and stuffed the shirt inside with the other.

"Probably better if I take all this mess with me when I go," he said.

"I agree. In fact it'd be best if you hadn't come at all, but you don't seem to get that message. Now sit down and let me get a look at that wound."

Harman sat in one of the aspen-log chairs that Shane had built for himself back when he worked for a local furniture maker who sold Adirondack chairs to tourists. Shane put on a pair of latex gloves and leaned in close to Harman's chest to get a look. It had to be the closest the two had been to each other in years. Shane nudged at the wound with just a fingertip, used a towel to dab at the area around it.

"What'd he stab you with, and how deep?" Shane asked.

"How you know it was a he?" Harman tried to smile, but Shane's face registered nothing. "Goddamn pocket knife. I was too busy trying to not get stuck again to bother seeing how deep it went in."

"You having any trouble breathing?"

"No more than usual. I still want a smoke, put it like that."

Shane rolled his eyes and started to put away the kit. "You're fine, Harman. It's a puncture wound, but it don't look all that deep. Besides, if they'd hit anything important you'd probably have bled out by now."

"So that's it?" Harman asked.

"What's it?"

"That's it, you're not going to bandage it, nothing like that? How you know it ain't serious?"

"I don't. I'm not a fucking doctor. You see an MRI

machine anywhere in this kitchen? From what I can tell you'll be alright, that's all I can say. It could probably use stitches, but good luck with that, I'm not taking it there."

"Can you at least bandage it for me?" Harmon asked.

"Keep some pressure on it for a while longer, until the bleeding stops. Here's some alcohol pads and gauze and tape to clean and cover it up. You can see to all that yourself. I think you should go to the hospital, but that's just me. Right now get it cleaned and covered, cause it's time to go."

"You're kicking me out?"

"I thought that much was clear up front," Shane said.

"Shane, I'm sorry, I really am. I know I've been a shitty father. But I've got nowhere else to go. Please don't put me out in the cold right now."

"I told you the deal, Harman. Get dressed and get gone. I still have to be out on the road in an hour and some change, regardless of what bullshit you've brought to my door. See yourself out. I'm going to start getting ready for work. Have a nice life." Shane turned and walked back into the darkened house toward the stairway that led up to the bedroom in the loft. He stopped at the foot of the stairs. "I mean it, Harman. Get a move on. It'd be nice if you decided to make something better of yourself, but there's no hope left for you around here." Shane's footsteps echoed in the quiet house as he climbed the stairs.

Harman cleaned and dressed the wound as best he could, then eased on the shirt Shane had given him, trying not to move his abdomen too much. He collected all the bloodied materials up into the trash bag and took it with him.

As he moved out the door he snagged an almost full bottle of Jack Daniels sitting on the shelf above the stove. He pulled his winter hat back on and hit the light switch on his way out into the night, not sure if he'd ever see his son again. He ought to let Shane move on, but for some reason he still struggled with it. He took a long pull from the whisky bottle once he settled into the driver's seat.

The worn out Subaru turned over a few times before the engine caught. He kept pressure on his wound with the left hand and alternated shifting and steering with the right. He'd almost forgotten about the body in the back. Almost.

Now that he felt confident he wasn't going to die, he decided to head west out of town. If he could make it through the drive around the reservoir and down into lower country where it probably wasn't snowing so much, he might find somewhere to ditch the body out in the high desert. Then he could make for Junction, get help at the hospital there maybe, and disappear west into some remote desert town to start over. Or maybe he was kidding himself.

Either way he had no other options. He couldn't come back here ever again, that much was certain.

The snow had eased up some. The roads were slick as hell on the way out of town. Whatever cops were on duty were probably huddled up somewhere warm, meaning the highway out around the reservoir ought to be empty, since most truckers wouldn't drive at night in a storm like this.

As he drove, the windshield started to fog again. By the time he'd driven ten miles to the point where the highway first hugged the reservoir's shore on his left, he could barely see. He knew he should lay off the whiskey, but it was helping with the sharp pain from the stab wound now, so he took another pull. Five more miles and the snow started up again in flurries. It would still be at least another fifteen miles before the road would even begin to slope down into lower elevation.

Harman squinted and tried to dig in the passenger floorboard for an ice scraper to chunk off the thin ice layer forming on the inside of the glass. He reached too far and winced as he felt blood spurt out from his wound. He looked up to see an elk cow's rough outline standing in the center of the highway. Out of instinct, he swerved away from the water onto the shoulder, then completely lost control.

The Subaru see-sawed back and forth until the rear passenger tire hit the snow piled up at the edge of the highway, sending the Subaru into a sideways barrel roll.

Harman's world swirled end over end. Somewhere in that death spin the windshield shattered and cold air rushed in to meet him. Harman's head slammed into the steering wheel as the car's side hammered into the thick granite wall about 200 feet off the highway, and he lost consciousness.

* * *

Harman woke again hanging upside down, unsure where he was or what had happened, his entire world inverted. It was only after he realized he was still buckled into his seatbelt with blood pooling on the car's ceiling below him that he remembered where he was.

It took him a moment to figure out how to unbuckle himself. When he managed to do so, he collapsed into the blood pool below him and something popped in his back. He couldn't move anymore after that, so he just lay there for what felt like a long time, looking out through the shattered windshield at the snowy sky, thinking he was either dead or caught, and not sure if he cared which one it was.

Flashing yellow lights appeared in his peripheral vision back on the highway. A moment later he heard feet crunching in the snow, but couldn't turn his head to see them. A flashlight appeared in his eyes.

"Harman?" a familiar voice said. "Goddammit. Harman, are you ok?" Harman couldn't place the voice for a moment, could not himself manage to speak. When the flashlight beam left his face to survey the wreckage around him Harman realized it was Shane. He tried to sit back up, but his body felt far away from him,. "Stay still, Harman," Shane said. "I radioed for help. Someone will be here soon."

Harman tried to move again. It took a lot of effort to even keep his eyes open. Finally he stopped trying and allowed himself to sink back into darkness.

* * *

He awoke again to find himself outside of the vehicle with two EMTs easing him onto an emergency stretcher.

"Is he the only victim?" One of them said.

"There's another one about fifty feet that way," Shane's voice said, though Harman couldn't tell where he was standing now. "Looks like the second one was ejected from the car when it flipped. I checked him but he was already gone." The EMTs nodded to each other. Shane went on. "Hard to believe Harman here was the smarter one, but he had his seatbelt on."

"You know this man?" One of the EMTs said.

"He's my father."

The EMTs looked at each other again. Harman tried to speak but his mouth wouldn't move. "Estranged father," Shane added, as if that changed something. "I hadn't seen him in months before he showed up a few hours ago at my back door. I shouldn't have turned him away in this weather, I don't know why I did that. I'm just sick of his shit, I guess. He must have picked up this other fella on the way out of town."

Shane's voice had regret in it. Harman understood that even in his diminished state. If he could speak, his own voice would too. Somewhere in that tone he could hear the love Shane had once had for him slipping out, perhaps without his son's permission.

As the men hoisted Harman up and carried him through the snow back to the side of the highway, Harman focused himself on that small, insignificant bit of love. It would turn into disgust again as soon as they figured out that Ray Miller's body had been strangled to death hours before it ever came to a rest on the side of that snowy highway.

But in this moment Harman let himself feel like the victim, like a father that a son might feel sorry to lose. Maybe the paramedics would shoot him up with some morphine on the way to the hospital. At least he still had that to look forward to.

EDICT FROM NOWHERE

YOU HEAR HORRIBLE THINGS here at night. Thirty-five years and I've never gotten used to the screams. There's so many things you see every day, degrading things, but it's the things you don't see, the things you can only hear while you try to sleep at night, that burrow deep inside you. Sometimes not even being able to put a face to the terror, only a name. Higgins. Clark. Johnson. All of them dead now. Each having traveled through twenty, thirty, forty years of living only to end up sodomized and dead on a filthy concrete floor.

When I first got in here I was scared to fucking death. I was thirty-five years old then, and I'm not too proud to admit I wept that first night. For the first couple of years I worked through every appeal there was. I still had dreams about life on the outside, my child back in her crib, my ex-wife standing on the sand of Stewart beach in Galveston on the day we got married, smiling.

I try not to think about those days anymore. You let people see weakness inside you here and they'll gut you like an animal. Won't be nothing left of you but a number, maybe a bloodstain on the bathroom floor. Every last ounce of your life wasted and dripping down a prison drain.

All you can do is get up, go to work in the laundry, or the fields, eat and sleep and shit alongside the rest of them. Some of them killers, but most just petty thieves and addicts.

The best strategy is to walk tall and keep to yourself. If you let these boys see there's a heart in your chest they'll make sure all you feel is pain. Most of them never learned how to feel much of anything decent anyhow. Blame who you want to for that.

I've watched a lot of men crack. You have to learn to let go. Seems like people are determined to let go of everything in their lives except the horror. So much beauty in life but nearly everyone ends up strangled by the ugly parts.

Most days feel like waiting for your turn. Some of them are men you've known for over twenty years before it happens. You learn to see it coming. They start to talk less, spend less time interacting on the yard. Sometimes they just lay on their bunks all day, glass eyes staring into the nothing ahead of them like looking for fish beneath the water's surface. Like the very thing that created them has finally been torn out.

Knowing that it's impossible to get away from all this cruelty can cause a man to abandon hope after a while. On the one hand maybe he regrets the things he's done in his life, on the other hand he sees that it doesn't make a load of horseshit to be sorry. Sorry is meaningless in here. If you tell someone you're sorry they'll just call you con artist. Liar. Killer. You'll see in their eyes how much they hate you for saying it.

My first cellmate Karl Sanders checked out by running up in the middle of the black's section of the yard screaming, "Niggers, niggers! All of you!" They stomped on his head until it burst like a rotten orange.

Darnell Watkins climbed the fence on the yard one afternoon and screamed "Get at me bitch!" to the guard in the tower. He was all tangled up in the razor wire on top of the fence when the first bullet hit, around his kidneys. He thrashed and moaned as the wires sawed into his skin and let out his blood. The second bullet smashed into his left shoulder and came out through his chest. He would've dropped down into the grass except he was all tangled up in the razor wire with blood streaking down his forearms in long scarlet streams that turned his white jump suit red. Darnell, he just hung there and bled out with a crazed, vacant smile on his face.

Others have hung themselves, cut their wrists with sharpened scraps of metal. Banged their heads on the cinder block walls until their minds were erased. Each one just another example of how much a man can come to resent the gift of life. There's no use even trying to understand that kind of loneliness unless you're forced to live with it. Which I am.

All of this hell spewing into your eyes every day gets to be too much. A man will wipe all memory of himself from this earth just to know he has something left to control. An existence that can be erased, even if his death means an anonymous grave in a hayfield out back of hell, no flowers, no headstone. The flowers would be an insult anyway. Death doesn't need company to be final.

I'm tired most all the time now. My joints and muscles throb from three-and-a-half decades of sleeping on a foam mat. If someone had told me the day I got here that I'd still be alive this far in, I'd have called them a fool. I didn't think I'd survive a week, yet here I am.

Every night I see the faces that have come and gone while I've remained. Faces consumed by violence and poor choices, but also destroyed by the hopelessness of incarceration.

Faces of men who dwelled on the past so long that it destroyed the present. Lifetimes of stories erased by the teller. Each of them alive in my mind and speaking their truths to me night after night, until they start to make sense in the worst kind of way.

DOO-DOO THE BIKER BOYEE

TRAVIS HAD BEEN OUT of prison for almost a month when he finally found work as a meat cutter at a neighborhood *bodega* called Thompson's on Twelfth Street.

The owner Manny was an ex-con, though most people didn't know that, and he had a soft spot for guys like Travis who were trying to put their lives back together. Travis wasn't a big fan of handling raw meat, but he needed to eat so he decided he'd get used to it.

Except it turned out he didn't get used to it, not for a while at least. By his third day on the job he was ready to say fuck it, collect the wages they owed him and go buy a bottle of Kentucky D, drink until parole came to lock him back up. The motorcycle ride to and from work each day was the only thing that kept him from actually doing that. He loved to ride that bike.

He'd built the old chopper himself off a salvaged title ten years ago and owned it outright. It was the only thing that remained of his life before they tossed his drunk ass in the pen for smashing a cop's teeth in at Randall's Cocktail Lounge when Travis was on maybe the third day or so of his last big bender.

That, and the scars on his forehead and chin he'd gotten after the officer's backup arrived and beat him unconscious. He still had some of those, too. He considered them built-in reminders that he didn't want to go back to prison, and so he couldn't drink ever again.

Travis had been riding and working on motorcycles since he was fourteen. Now that he was sober and trying to straighten his life up, it gave him more comfort than ever to be out on the open road with wind tearing through the greasy shag-carpet hair that hung off his head. When he got his first check he planned to take a long ride out of the city and get his first look in almost five years at wide-open countryside that wasn't beyond a barbed wire fence.

But only if he could survive a full week at his nasty new job. Which he somehow managed to do, in spite of how nauseous it made him.

That first Friday afternoon he was packaging ground beef and thinking about a fifth of Kentucky Deluxe again when someone rang the bell out at the counter. He weighed out one more pound on a Styrofoam tray, wrapped it in saran wrap, and slapped the label that automatically printed out from the scale onto the front.

He tossed his gloves in the trash and washed his hands, then stepped out the swinging doors to find himself face-to-face with a pair of the most beautiful green eyes he'd ever seen. The woman behind them blushed and pushed a lock of curly auburn hair behind her ear when she noticed the stupefied look on Travis's face. He shook himself out of the shock and greeted her with a chipper "May I help you, ma'am?"

"Ma'am?" she replied. "I think you're looking for my mother. You can call me Lynn, *mister*."

"I see," Travis said, trying to straighten himself up without moving, to get his voice nice and even. "I guess you can call me Travis, then." He pointed at his nametag as he said it, felt like a moron right away for doing so. "What can I do for you, Miss Lynn?"

He flirted with her some more as she ordered a top sirloin and a link of spicy Italian sausage, and it surprised him when she flirted back. During the time he'd been locked up he couldn't even picture a woman so beautiful. He tried to be funny, and it seemed to work. She laughed at all his jokes. She stood there talking to him long after he packaged up her order and handed it over.

By the end of the conversation she doubled her order and made him promise to come over and cook it all for her.

From that moment on he didn't mind cutting meat anymore. He hadn't complained to himself about it once in the three months he'd been dating Lynn since having that first dinner together.

Barely a week after that first date he'd started staying over at her place instead of at the halfway house where his mattress smelled like piss and nobody paid much attention to his comings and goings anyway. He'd just roll through the office at night to check in, then walk right out the back door, hop the fence, and ride off on his bike to Lynn's place.

Things were moving fast. When he told her about prison she didn't even blink, just nodded her head like she understood exactly what it had been like for him.

After work every night he'd pick her up and they'd cruise around town on the chopper, and never once did he even think about stopping to have a drink. Both the relationship and the job had gone like that every second of those first three months together afterward, no bumps, just peaceful. It was the first time in his life he could remember feeling at peace.

Travis started to live stable, too. No biker gangs, no drugs, and most of all, no blacking out on whiskey and beating someone half to death.

When Lynn suggested it was time for him to meet her family, Travis hesitated. Why? She'd already told him her brother was a lawyer who thought he knew everything, and her mother was some sort of Xanax-soaked socialite, who spent most afternoons digging into other peoples' business from the bottom thrid of a wine bottle.

Though he assumed she was just being hard on her family the way people usually are, he was more afraid of what they might think of him. Lynn didn't spend much time dealing with either of them, and yet she felt very strong that he needed to meet them if she were going to continue seeing him so seriously.

So Travis relented and agreed to come to her brother's family birthday dinner the next week.

They rode the chopper across town after Travis got off work. Lynn directed him through the suburban neighborhoods and cookie cutter subdivisions until they pulled to a stop in front of a two-story white-brick house with colorful flowers in the flowerbeds and the cleanest, greenest lawn Travis had ever seen. Travis killed the engine and took off his helmet. Lynn had already climbed off the bike.

"You sure it's alright if I come along?" Travis asked, wanting to gesture all around him for some reason, as if to ask what he was supposed to do in a place like that.

"Of course," Lynn assured him, "stop worrying. I told you, daddy rode bikes too. My mother likes motorcycles." Travis didn't have the heart to tell her that he only needed one look at the house to know that the way her father had ridden bikes was not the same way he rode them. Or used to ride them, anyway.

It wasn't his bike or the way he looked that he was worried about so much as the time he'd spent in prison. He couldn't imagine a parent being happy to hear that about their daughter's new boyfriend.

He let it drop and followed her up the flower-lined sidewalk to the front door. For some reason he expected her to knock, was shocked to see that the door was unlocked when she just turned the knob and walked right in. Travis hesitated at the threshold for so long that Lynn had to pull him inside the rest of the way.

"Come on you big goon," she giggled. Her smile melted whatever anxiety he was feeling away, like always. He'd never been with someone who made him feel like that. Even his own mother had spent most of her time scowling at him or downright ignoring him when she got into one or another of her drunken stupors. Being with Lynn was really helping him to understand how calming a woman's love could be.

"Lynn baby, is that you?" a woman's voice called

45

from beyond the entry hall.

"Hi mom, it is," Lynn said, leading Travis by the hand. Her mother appeared in the doorframe to the kitchen wearing a blue sundress probably made for women half her age, though she filled it out pretty well. She had long red nails and a set of pearls around her neck. She wore a big straw sunhat that could cast a two-foot diameter patch of shade onto her face.

"You must be Travis," the gaudy woman said, extending her dainty hand to him. "I'm Patty. We've heard so much about you."

Travis forced a nervous smile and gave her hand a soft shake. "It's a pleasure, ma'am," he replied. "I've heard a lot about you as well."

"All good things I hope," Patty said, her eyes watching Lynn's face for a reaction.

"Of course." Travis let her hand go and she moved to let him and Lynn pass.

"Well color me surprised, then. Old mom has always been a bit of an embarrassment around here." Patty smiled to show she was joking.

Lynn flinched for a half second, then erased it from her face. But it was enough to tell Travis that the comment stung. He was proud of her when she managed to ignore it. No one in his family had ever ignored anything that wasn't a bill. Patty started to say something else, but the front door opened with a lot of commotion.

"Knock, knock," a man's voice called out. "Mom, we're here."

"How perfect," Patty said. "Timothy's here on time, for once."

A boy of five or six pushed his way between Tim's legs and ran down the hallway into Patty's arms.

"Grandma," he called out as she swept him up.

"Hello Carson," she said. "So glad you made it. But what have I told you? Call me Gigi, sweetheart, not Grandma."

"Ok Gigi, I forgot." Carson's eyes met Travis's and Travis smiled at him. Carson buried his face into Patty's shoulder, suddenly self-conscious now that he realized there were strangers around.

"Hi Carson," Lynn said. Carson shot her a look and then buried his face in Patty's shoulder again.

"He gets shy around strangers at first," Lynn explained. "But he'll be all over you in a minute." Patty put the boy down as Tim came into the room putting his cell phone into the front pocket of his suit coat.

"*Hello* Birthday Boy," Patty cooed.

"Hi mom," he said. "Thanks. Sorry, that was a client. What can I say, business is booming." He met Travis's eyes then. "So you must be the mysterious Travis?"

Travis nodded and extended his hand. "I don't know that there's much mystery to me, but I am Travis."

Tim looked at his hand but didn't shake it. When Travis realized he probably wasn't going to, he took it back and put it in his pocket.

Tim said: "So what's for dinner, Ma? I'm starving."

"Baked ziti with some garlic bread and a bottle of Twomey Merlot Francine is featuring this month in the wine club. You'll like it. Do you drink red wine, Travis?"

Travis might have smiled involuntarily if he hadn't seen alarm on Lynn's face. Instead he tried to seem relaxed. "Never had much of it, honestly," he said. "A little Rossi here and there. But that's okay, actually. I don't drink."

Patty looked as if she'd never heard of such a thing. She seemed to rearrange her face before she replied, "Oh. Well, that's alright. Is there something you'd rather drink with dinner instead, maybe some milk?"

"No, thank you ma'am. Water would be fine."

"Well if you'll excuse me a moment, I need to put the garlic bread in the oven." Patty sauntered off to the kitchen.

"Daddy," Carson said, pulling at the bottom of Tim's suit coat. "Can I got out back and play now?"

Tim looked at the boy's hands on the bottom of his suit as if waiting for Carson to let go before he would speak, then said, "Sure, son. But stay up on the porch, no further. And *be careful*."

Carson smiled and sped out the back door. Tim turned back to face Travis.

"So no booze, huh? What'd you do to end up on the wagon?"

"Inappropriate question, Tim," Lynn broke in.

"I don't mind," Travis said, measuring his words. "Not the first time I've been asked about it, won't be the last. Let's just say alcohol doesn't make me the best version of myself. I've made some mistakes and paid the price, so I don't figure on having to relearn them. I stay away from booze, and in exchange I get to be the real me."

"I see," Tim said, a bit of a smirk coming across his face. "If you don't mind my asking, did the real you have to do some time to figure all that out?"

"Matter of fact he did. I guess it must be that

obvious."

"Not really, just a hunch," Tim said, shifting his focus to Lynn. "Surely you're not gonna tell mom, she'll have a conniption."

"Tell mom what?" Patty said. "Bread's in the oven, dinner in ten minutes, by the way."

"Tim was just joking around with Travis about something. *Right* Tim?" Lynn bored a hole through Tim with her eyes. Tim nodded in agreement. "Speaking of which," Lynn added, "can I chat with you real quick in the living room, Tim?"

Patty wrung her hands. "I'll just be in the kitchen. Travis can I bring you anything?"

"No thanks," Travis said. "I'm good. Think I'll just step out back and have a smoke, if that's okay."

Patty looked like she might roll her eyes, but didn't. "Of course," she replied.

"I'll be right out, Trav," Lynn said as she took Tim by the arm and led him into the living room. Travis went out the back door onto the large covered back porch, which was elevated by a concrete staircase above the rest of the back yard. Carson was riding a bicycle with training wheels in circles around the porch while making fart noises with his mouth in imitation of a motorcycle engine.

"Whatcha up to there, bud?" Travis asked as he lit his smoke.

Carson looked him over but kept riding around making the fart sounds instead of responding.

Travis shrugged and puffed on his cigarette, looked over the back yard, which looked like it had once had a swimming pool that had since been filled in and covered with grass. A full minute had gone by before Carson pulled up next to Travis and stopped making the noise.

"I'm riding motorcycles," he said. "Like my grandpa did back before he went to heaven."

Travis smiled down at the boy. "I ride motorcycles too," he said. "Matter of fact, you might have seen my motorcycle out front of the house when you came in. Me and your aunt Lynn come over on it together, actually."

"Really?"

"Really. Maybe in a little while we can go out there and give it a look, if ya want."

"That would be awesome," Carson said, then frowned. "If my dad will let me. My friend Ralph has this toy, it's called Doo-Doo the Biker. You can use a remote control to drive him and he rides around on his motorcycle going pllllllllppppppppppp." Carson made the fart noises with his mouth again for effect, then added, "I was riding my bike just now to imitate him."

"Wow, that must be quite a toy. Not sure I've ever seen one of those." Travis forced another smile, not sure how to take the kid now.

"It's awesome, at least Ralph says it is. His mom won't let him bring it over to our house because it costs too much, and my dad doesn't allow me to go over to their house, so I never got to play with it yet."

"It sounds great," Travis said, thinking no way that toy existed. "Maybe you will sometime."

"Yeah, maybe. Anyhow he can do stunts and jump off stuff, and when you pull the string on his back he says 'I'm Doo-Doo the Biker BOYEE!' and then speeds off to do more tricks and stuff." Carson laid into his bike pedals as a demonstration and took off full force making the fart sound with his mouth again. He swiveled his head to make sure Travis was watching him go.

Watch out," Travis said, reaching out into empty space in front of him as if to pick the boy up, who was already well out of his reach. Carson ignored him and grinned, was pedaling full force when his front wheel left the porch's top step and sent him sailing out over the concrete pad below. Travis caught just a hint of panic in the boy's eyes before he inverted and his face disappeared from view. Carson landed with a dull thud on the concrete and everything went quiet for a half second, then the silence was filled with a deep animal moan, then outright sobbing and tears.

Travis reached the bottom of the stairs before the door into the house was even open. Carson was laying on his side on the concrete below curled up and hugging his knees, which were both skinned up.

The sight of blood made Travis's own knees go weak, brought back memories of the officer he'd nearly beaten to death. It still amazed him that he could have done something like that. He shook off the thought and knelt down over Carson, who was crying so hard now that no more sound came out.

"Where's it hurt, bud?" Travis asked, unable to think of anything else to say. Carson stared at him as if from far away, didn't speak.

"Get the fuck away from him," Tim screamed from behind Travis. Travis turned just in time to duck a sucker punch. He bent over at the waist and Tim's momentum sent him sailing over the top of Travis to land on top Carson, who managed an audible shriek again then.

"What the hell is going on?" Patty, who Travis had not seen appear, asked.

"Travis what happened?" Lynn said, alarmed.

"He was riding his bike but not looking where—" Travis started to say, but Tim cut him off.

"I'll tell you what happened. This crazy son of a bitch was out here abusing Carson, that's what. Tim stood up as if to lunge at Travis. Travis held his hands up in front of him and backed away. "I knew he was trouble as soon as I saw him, Mom," Tim said, turning now to address Patty. "Did you know he's been to *prison*? He'll be going back when I'm through with him."

Patty, who was attending to Carson now, gasped at the word *prison* and stared at Travis in horror. Travis shook his head yes, then no, then looked at Lynn, helpless, unsure which was right. Patty tried to ask Carson what had happened, but the boy gave her the same silent, desperate look he'd given Travis.

"That has nothing to do with any of this," Lynn said to Tim, then turned back to Travis. "Travis, tell us what happened."

"I was out here smoking and Carson was riding his bike. We had a little chat about motorcycles and he was showing me how he can ride, telling me about his friend Ralph has a toy called … well, anyway, he was telling me about Ralph's toy. He was riding without looking in front of him and rode right off the stairs before I could stop him. I think the poor little dude's got some Knievel in him." Travis grinned to show he was joking. No one else smiled back. He was trying to think of what to say next when the smoke alarm erupted from the open door to the house.

"Shit," Patty said, cradling Carson in her arms, who was latched on to her like a monkey now. "I forgot about the garlic bread. Hurry Timmy, go get it out of the oven for me."

"I'm not leaving him here alone with my son," Tim snarled, gesturing at Travis. "I don't care what he says, he was trying to hurt Carson, I know it. Carson wouldn't just ride off the stairs like that."

Travis almost replied to Tim but thought better. Instead he decided to take action. "Be right back," he called over his shoulder as he sprinted off into the house.

"Great, now he's fleeing the scene," Tim said.

Travis ignored him as he blew past the threshold with Lynn on his heels, into the smoky kitchen. Smoke was seeping from the oven. The sound of the alarm made it hard to hear anything else.

"Where are the oven mitts?" he yelled to Lynn over his shoulder.

"Top drawer to the left of the oven," Lynn yelled back.

Travis found two oven mitts and whipped the oven open. He took a cloud of smoke to the dome for his troubles, but he pulled the baking sheet of charred black bread chunks out and made his way back outside and down the steps. He set it down on the concrete and they all congregated around it like a campfire, even Carson, who was on his own two feet now.

"*Damn it*," Patty said, putting her hands on her hips like a pouty child.

Tim was knelt down attending to Carson, who seemed no worse for the wear, overall. "Did this man push you off the stairs?" Tim asked, cupping Carson by the shoulders and ignoring the smoking pan of charred bread. "Tell me what happened," he coaxed.

"I was riding my bike and I rode off the stairs,"

Carson said. "I guess I did a stunt kind of like Doo Doo the Biker." He grinned at Travis, already forgetting the fear of it.

"Like Doo-Doo the What? What's he talking about?" Tim said, glaring up at Travis now.

"Like I told you, bud. He was telling me about his friend's toy. Doo-Doo the Biker is his friend's toy. I can't believe you thought I'd push a kid off the stairs. I done a lot of things in my life, and we can talk about all of them, if you want. But I wouldn't hurt a kid. Specially not a fellow rider at heart like this little guy." Travis winked at Carson, and Carson smiled again through his still-wet eyes.

"You see, Tim?" Lynn butted in. "See how you're always overreacting to everything? He's a kid. They get bumps and scrapes, it happens. Travis didn't do anything, in fact he was helping Carson and you tried to punch his face in for the trouble."

Tim stood up and puffed his chest out at her. "If you're asking me to apologize for protecting my son, you can go ahead and can it, cause I don't want to hear it."

"I'm asking you to apologize for trying to punch *Travis*," Lynn snapped, starting to get angry now. Travis put his hand on her back as if to slow her down. She shrugged it off. Patty was too busy obsessing over the burned garlic bread to add to the disagreement.

"Well?" Lynn said, crossing her arms and tapping her foot.

"Well, what?" Tim replied.

"Are you going to tell Travis you're sorry, or not? He could have mangled you if he wanted. You should be begging his forgiveness and thanking him for his patience."

"That's not necessary," Travis said.

Tim's cell phone started ringing, saving him from a response. He dug it out of his pocket, clearly happy to have something to get him out of the discussion. One look at the screen and he mumbled, "I've gotta take this," then walked off toward the house as he projected a chipper "hello?"

"Really?" Lynn said. "That's great. This is all just fucking great."

"Sweetheart, language," Patty said. "Carson is still here."

"Yeah, well we're not," Lynn barked. "Come on Travis, let's go." She took Travis by the arm as if to lead him away, but he shook off her grip. "Travis?" she said, confused.

"Not necessary," Travis said, "I think we can manage a meal without garlic bread, and it looks like the misunderstanding's all cleared up, no? How about this—everybody come inside and sit down to dinner and I'll tell you all about how I messed my life up and went to prison. Parts of it are funny, actually. To tell you the truth, I was nervous coming here today because I thought you all would think my people must be crazy for me to end up how I did. Now I can see I'm in good company." Travis smiled, had to stifle a laugh at his own joke.

No one said anything to that, and he thought for a second the joke might have been too much. They all stood there trying not to look at each other until Tim came back outside just as he was hanging up the phone call.

"So, should we eat?" he asked, acting as if nothing had happened at all. Patty smiled and headed off into the house with Tim right behind her.

Lynn studied Travis for his reaction and he winked at her. She pulled him in close to her and gave him a big kiss. "Thank you," she said. "Thank you, thank you, thank you."

"For what?" Travis replied.

"For being you," Lynn said.

Travis smiled and winked at her again.

"Well, who else would I be?" he asked.

EYE OF THE HURRICANE

TERRANCE STANDS BEFORE HIS grandmother Irma's grave, a woman he barely remembers from his childhood. The mid-day sun above him boils everything below it in sticky waves of humidity that feel like a smothering wet blanket has been dropped on top of his life.

He only has a single memory of Irma, from a brief period when he lived with her as a toddler. Just before his third birthday his mother had sent him to Irma after his father left them for the last time. A tiny Terrance watching as Irma rifles through the sale racks of clothing at a mall, every now and then scanning the aisles around her and then stuffing something she wants into her giant purse.

There's nothing spectacular about the memory except that it's the only one Terrance can recall of this woman he'll soon be buried next to. Terrance has never stolen anything himself. Not just yet.

Terrance is afraid, no question about that. What scares him more than anything else is the loss of his presence as a living, conscious being. That there might be nothing, and everything that entails. But it's more than that, too. He doesn't want to leave a hole in his family, doesn't want them to suffer from his absence.

When he received his first cancer diagnosis two years ago, such thoughts only served to make him afraid. But that time he'd gotten better, and healing had made him hopeful. The chemo and countless nights of pain and suffering had achieved something, and it had made him a better man in the process, a better husband and father with a second chance at making a good life for his family.

When he got the news two months ago that the cancer had returned, it was like all of those feelings evaporated, but especially his sense of hope. Something in him realized that it came down to acceptance, nothing more. He was going to die this time, like it or not. But that didn't stop the fear he felt for his family.

A new specialist, one he hadn't worked with before, delivered him the confirmation that his gut feeling had been correct. The man looked straight into his eyes as he explained that the cancer had metastasized to his lymph nodes. That there was a sprawling tumor where one lung had once been, the reason he had been feeling short of breath.

The specialist, whose name Terrance forgot almost before he heard it, would have made a great poker player. His face stayed so unaffected throughout the conversation. Even his hand felt cold when Terrance shook it.

Afterwards Terrance had walked to a park near the hospital and wandered around it, trying to come to terms with what might become of his wife and child. The overcast sky was pregnant with dark clouds, and the air smelled like rain.

The only other person in the park sat on one of the stone benches arranged around the pond in the park's center. An old man casting a red-and-white bobber into a pond that Terrance had always assumed didn't have any fish in it.

He'd wandered past the man, deeper into the park. He sat on a log near the creek for what felt like hours and thought about what he should do next, what he might do for his family in the short time he had left on earth. It was there, alone and desperate on that log, worrying about Shirley and Lulu, that he'd first decided to rob a bank.

By the time Terrance had arrived home that night his mind was made up. Seeing Shirley and sweet, feeble-minded Lulu huddled there together at the kitchen table, waiting for him, nearly tore the heart out of his chest.

Shirley stood up and hugged him, and then Lulu joined her, the two of them pressing him into their center tight, so that he felt like the eye of a hurricane. In that moment he knew he had to do something for them, had to come up with a plan and execute it. Not just for the money. For balance. To balance the scales. He'd been a good man these last few years, only to end up like this.

The wind picks up and shakes Terrance from this world of thoughts and memory. He stands up from in front of Irma's grave and limps back across the graveyard to his truck. He fires up the engine and drives out of the parking lot, focused now on what he's about to do.

* * *

He drives thirty miles down the highway to Jacksonville, pulls into the strip mall on the far end of town, away from the main road, where a rear entrance leads out the back into a neighborhood.

He parks with the truck facing that exit, a straight shot out. He's taking a risk, having to cover about fifty yards on foot in his depleted condition, but that can't be helped. This is the quickest way out, through the decaying neighborhood and then a straight shot out onto Highway 69 out of town.

He opens the glove box and takes out the .38 snub nose revolver his father gave him when he was running wire line out in West Texas just after high school, puts it in the pocket of his duster coat. He tosses his wallet in and slams the glove box shut.

He eases his black Stetson hat off the passenger seat and sets it low on his head to cover his eyes. Then he climbs out of the truck, leaving it running, and limps his way across the parking lot into the Jacksonville First State Bank.

* * *

Fifteen minutes later he's still wheezing and trying not to black out from hyperventilation as the truck rolls down Highway 69. By the time he gets onto 346 he has to focus almost exclusively on breathing.

Somehow he manages to make it to the cemetery, pulls in and parks in the exact same spot he'd parked in not ninety minutes before. Back before he'd become a criminal. Back before it had only taken fifteen minutes to subtract all the lies he'd spent the last few years adding up and telling to himself. Once he calms down enough, he opens the green bank bag and counts the take.

Five-grand and some change. For some reason he had thought it would be more, though that assumption hadn't been based on any real-world information or experience. The teller had seemed so panicked when he set the gun on the counter. He could see in her eyes what a criminal piece of scum she thought he was. Even though there was no guard at the door he'd snatched the bag back from her as soon as she finished with the big bills and hustled to the exit, wanting to get away from that look.

Shit. Five thousand isn't even enough to do much for Shirley, for Lulu. He wishes it were more, but the truth is it is more than enough to establish what kind of man he will die as. Not that it matters, really.

Right now, he needs to get home before Shirley calls the cops and reports him missing. The last thing he needs is any interaction with law enforcement. Even thinking about police makes him paranoid.

Terrance rolls the money into a wad, gets out of the truck and limps over to Irma's grave. He hides it in the old, fading flower urn, then replaces the dead flowers on top of it. He breathes with a bit more relief, but he still has to sit there for a moment to catch his breath before making his way back to the truck to drive home.

* * *

When he gets there, Shirley and Lulu are waiting for him at the table again. Shirley looks angry, but she won't say it. She thinks he shouldn't be out of the house anymore. It's a feeble suggestion made by Dr. Roberts on his last visit, aimed at providing him with a few extra days to suffer. He'd just as soon die now as lie around suffering.

"You can't just do things like that," Shirley says, her eyes frantic but her voice calm. "You need your strength now more than ever."

Terrance frowns and wonders what coming horrors he should want to save his strength for. His Lulu sits and listens to their conversation as if she can understand it, as if the person inside her is as grown up as her body. But inside that nineteen-year-old body she's a child, will always be a child.

She doesn't really understand what's happening to him, to any of them, for that matter. This is good, Terrance has decided. Even if she had the ability to try and make sense of it she would fail, because there's no meaning to be found in dying from cancer.

Shirley helps him to the bedroom, then helps him out of his clothes. As her soft hands undress him he reflects on the way people are always so gentle with him now. Like if they make too much commotion he'll keel over and die. His entire life he's spent working like a dog under the Texas sun, and now he's too soft to be touched like man. He's decided that this is the worst part of dying slow: it makes everyone else so goddamned hesitant and nervous.

Shirley kisses him on the forehead and tucks him under the covers. He knows she still understands him as the strong, able man she married, that this person laying here confuses her, so he lets it go. As she clicks off the light he sees the fatigue in her eyes, though she forces a smile for his sake.

She whispers "goodnight," then it's dark and he watches the ceiling fan wander circles around the ceiling, coercing him to sleep along to the sound of his wheezes and coughs.

* * *

Late that night things get much worse than he has anticipated. He wakes up with an intense burning in his chest and abdomen. His breath comes in gasps. It feels like someone is pressing down on his chest with all their weight.

He reaches for them, but no one's there. Shirley hears the movement and wakes up almost immediately. She cradles his head and rocks back and forth, whispers through her tears that he will be all right. Even though he won't, and she knows that he knows she knows it. These attacks have gotten worse every night for two weeks. This is the first one that truly scares Terrance too.

He cannot breathe. He. Cannot. Breathe. HE CANNOT BREATHE.

Through his panic he sees Lulu, still half asleep, standing in the doorway in red flannel footie pajamas, outlined in a silhouette of light that seems intentional. Shirley says something and Lulu disappears. She returns holding the pre-fixed syringe the doctors prescribed for them in case this happened.

It's like Shirley can't get the needle out fast enough. Terrance shakes, coughs, chokes. For a moment he thinks this is the end. The needle feels hot in his arm and its warmth permeates the rest of his body in a soothing wave. His breath comes to him again in gasps. He slides back into sleep again.

* * *

The following morning the worker from hospice, a heavy-set woman named Marie with curly brown hair, arrives to help with administering the morphine that's supposed to comfort him on the way out. She's cheerful with a high-pitched laugh, and he likes her right away because he sees there's no pity in her eyes when she looks at him.

He figures it's because she's done this too many times by now — the effect isn't the same as it once was. She's there when he wakes up that morning, and also when he goes to sleep that afternoon. This comforts him, because there's nothing at stake for her here but the loss of a stranger's life. He has no ability to harm her on his way out.

It allows him to spend a moment or two every so often feeling like he did before the cancer returned: casual. People are never casual about cancer, and this only makes it more terrifying.

The day after Marie first arrives they're sitting in his room chatting about basketball in a moment when Terrance is awake. He's too weak now to get out of bed. He might never leave this room again, though not if he can help it. But things are calm just now.

Marie sits in a chair pulled up next to the bed and reads him an article from the paper about the Dallas Mavericks' game the night before. He thinks about the game he went to a month after the cancer resurfaced, one of many things that had been on his "things-to-get-done-before-death" list. By then he was already looking sick as hell, but it had been fun for the most part.

A friend arranged for front-row tickets and a limo

ride to and from the game. Shirley and Lulu accompanied him even though they didn't care much about basketball.

Terrance had already grown weaker then, but they managed a good time of it, he decides now. Shirley must have sensed how naked he felt in his translucent skin, because she stuck to his arm the whole night, and it felt good to have his wife on his arm. He would miss that as much as anything about being alive.

After the game they went into the locker area by showing their VIP stubs. As they stood there taking pictures with a few of the players Terrance couldn't shake the feeling that everyone was staring at him. As soon as he came in he noticed a change in the room.

The way people's eyes softened when they looked at him, like one rough look might put him down. This nearly destroyed him, but he kept it inside. He didn't like feeling weak that way, not then any more than he does now. They left a short time after that, and he puked into a bag the entire ride home while Shirley rubbed the back of his neck.

Marie says something that he misses and he looks at her dreamily from the morphine drip. "What was that?" he whispers.

"I said someone robbed a bank in Jacksonville yesterday," she repeats. "Can you believe that?"

"Oh." Terrance pauses, remembers the money and tries to sit up. Marie just puts a hand on his chest, guides him back down.

"Relax, Mr. Terrance," she says. "No need to be getting all worked up over some thief taking money from some big bad bank."

Terrance relaxes, too weak to resist her. He wants

to say more, has an inclination to share his secret with her because of the drugs, but the words won't come.

She smiles. "You just sit back and rest," she says, and tucks the covers tighter around his chest.

That night, after Shirley gets home from the store and Marie goes off duty, Terrance drags himself to his feet and puts on a coat. He needs to get the money, if he can. It's worth maybe dying to get it, even. Shirley is downstairs cooking. Lulu isn't back from Special Needs school yet. They've agreed not to interrupt her life any more than they have to over this thing.

If he's careful he can slip out unnoticed, maybe manage to pick the money up and get back in bed before Shirley realizes he's gone. He stumbles on the stairway and worries that Shirley might have heard him, has to wait there until he catches his breath to keep moving. It takes him two more stops like this before he's behind the wheel of his truck backing down the driveway.

Out on the street he drives the speed limit the five miles to the cemetery, wheezing for air the entire way. It's a wonder he doesn't black out behind the wheel, but somehow he manages to turn back in and park there in front of Irma's grave. The problem is, he can barely sit up straight, has to rest and try to stay conscious for five minutes before he even manages to get out of the truck.

It takes another five minutes sitting there in front of the grave, where he pockets the money, before he manages to get himself back into the truck and shut the door behind him. After that he drifts off to sleep from the morphine, can't tell how much time has gone by when he comes back into consciousness.

He starts the engine but is only able to drive at

half the speed limit home. Nobody seems to notice that on the road, or at least no one messes with him. When he pulls into the driveway there are other cars there, some he recognizes and some he doesn't. Shirley comes running out of the house just as he shuts off the engine, races toward him as he attempts to get out of the truck.

All he can manage is to get the door open enough to fall out onto the concrete. Shirley gasps as he tries to say something. Everything fades into black as he slips back out of consciousness again.

* * *

He wakes up back in bed, not sure how he has gotten there. The burning in his chest is more astringent now; each breath comes as a rattle. Even with the oxygen tank strapped on him he still has difficulty getting enough air. His breath comes now in crackling sobs, bursts of wheezing followed by a brooding silence, then, at the last second, more bursts. He can no longer speak when he tries.

There are people all around him in the room. They seem desperate to be near him now. His cousin Bobby is there, and so is Shirley's sister Gina, as well as two preachers apparently in competition for his soul. All of them have death in their wet eyes when they look at him.

He's so drugged he can't really move or keep his eyes open. Terrance listens with his eyes closed as they tell stories from his past. They tell them to each other in tiny voices, like saying them too loud will destroy them. It feels good to remember he has a past, and that it will remain in the absence of a future.

He would just let go and float away from all of it

now, but he's still afraid to leave Shirley and Lulu behind. He can't imagine her caring for Lulu all by herself, getting old like that with no one to understand the burden any more than to understand how worthwhile it is to carry it. He desperately wants to tell Shirley about the money, to let her know that he left her with something, howver small. The pain has become so widespread now that he cannot determine its origin anymore; only that it seems to have no end in its intensity and brutality.

People in the room speak of him as though he's already lost his perception. Terrance fades into sleep with his breath still rattling out of his chest.

* * *

Sometime in the night Terrance becomes aware of Shirley leaning over him, stroking his hair. Her tears drip on his forehead like hot salty raindrops. This overwhelms him because he can't move to comfort her.

The end feels near, but he struggles to hold on to his presence, to the essence of himself as a living, breathing being. After a long time she leans in close, stroking the thin hair above his ear as she whispers into it.

"It's okay now Terrance, you can let go," she says. "You don't have to stay here and suffer anymore. God is waiting for you."

Her tears feel like little bits of boiling water now as they land. Terrance decided a while ago that there is no god, nothing beyond this life. Considering the circumstances, this feels satisfactory to him now.

Terrance remembers the money again, knows it's not enough, but he needs for Shirley to have it, for her to know that he tried, at least. He forces his eyes open again. Shirley is there, and his cousin Bobby, and his wife Gina, who is hugging Lulu from behind, snuggling her for comfort. They're all blurry and a bit misshapen because Terrance can't quite get his eyes open all the way.

His body feels heavy and distant, and he knows the life is draining out of it now. He looks toward each of them and they're scared, this is evident even without focus.

He tries to smile at Lulu, but that kind of movement has already left him. He concentrates, now harder, now *harder*, finally manages to raise his left hand a little above the sheets. Everyone watches him and it feels like being on a stage, like a last performance.

He points at his duster, hanging on the rack by the doorway. He points at the duster and moans until Shirley figures out what he wants, retrieves it from the rack and brings it over, sits on the edge of the bed with it.

He moans, then again, somehow wills his right hand to reach out and flip open the front of the coat, to reveal the bulge in it. He takes Shirley's hand, uses his last bit of strength to place it on the lump. He watches through blurry slits as she takes the wad out of the coat, holds it in front of her face.

"Where did this come from?" she wonders out loud.

He wants to answer her but he's got nothing left, feels himself untethering from this reality. Instead he just closes his eyes and relaxes his mind, finally surrenders to this fate, finally lets go of it all.

FRANKLIN AND THE FINGER

FRANKLN USED A HANDKERCHIEF to hold the pale little lump between his index finger and thumb while he examined it. Only after he caught his own reflection in the mirror, mouth agape and holding the morbid thing, did it occur to him that he should call and let someone official know what he'd found. The problem was, that conversation kept going wrong in his head. He couldn't get past the ridiculousness of the situation to make the call.

"You found what in a coat?" The operator would say.

"A finger. Someone dropped the coat off in our overnight bin."

"And this is your coat? Sir, why do you have someone's finger in your coat?"

"Not my coat, a coat someone put in our night

return box. This is Bill's Haberdashery, down on Fifth Street. We rent out formal wears."

"Would you like me to send out an ambulance, sir?"

"No. Aren't you listening? There are no injured people here now, why would you send an ambulance?"

"Sir. Calm down."

"I'm calm. I just don't know what to do, and it seems to me someone has committed some sort of crime."

"Ok, I'll send out a unit." The operator would sigh and hang up at the end of the imagined conversation. Her attitude reminded Franklin of his ex-wife Jennifer. Always annoyed.

The finger had no blood on it, and had shriveled since detaching from the unfortunate individual it once belonged to. The suit coat he found it in had no traces of blood on it either. This lack of blood further made Franklin hesitate to call the police, as if the severed finger represented nothing more than some misunderstanding that would clear itself up in time, with or without his intervention.

The bell on the front door chimed, and a teenage girl with braided blonde hair stepped into the shop. She had a dress bag draped over her left arm.

"Hi, I'd like to return this dress—" she started to say, but her mouth fell open as her eyes met Franklin's at the finger held up in front of his face.

"Is that a fucking finger?" she blurted out, dropping the dress bag at her feet.

"It's, I—"

"Why the fuck do you have someone's finger?" she went on. "Holy shit. You're like, some creep murderer or something. I just wanted to return this dress. I didn't see anything, I swear."

"I didn't kill anybody," Franklin said, realizing how creepy and guilty it sounded only after he'd already said it.

"Then why do you have someone's finger?"

"I found it in a suit coat from our night depository. I was just about to call the authorities."

"It didn't look like you were calling the authorities to me. It looked like you were about to like, eat it or something. That's *fucked* up. Look, I didn't mean to interrupt whatever it is you're doing. I just wanted to bring back my prom dress. Please don't eat my fingers."

"I'm not gonna ... I don't eat fingers," Franklin replied, losing his calm now.

"What, you just eat the toes or something? I watched a show last week about foot obsessions, actually. It's called podophilia. None of the cases on the show were so bad they at the toes, though."

"I don't eat toes," Franklin snapped, and immediately wished that he hadn't, because it made him sound both aggressive and insane. The girl sucked in her breath and drew back as if to make for the door, then relaxed a little, stood still.

"So you really found it in one of the suits?" she asked.

"Yes, really. To be honest, I can't believe I'm actually touching it."

"It's so ... cool," she said. "Can I touch it too?" She picked the dress up, walked over and dropped it on the counter.

"Can you what? Why would you want to touch it?"

MICHAEL POOL

The girl shrugged. "I don't know. It's like, something out of a TV show or something."

She leaned in so that her eye was right next to the severed end of the finger.

"Wow, that thing is like totally for real. Megan will so freak out when she sees this. I gotta Instagram this for sure, hashtag *no filter*." She produced a cell phone from her pocket and snapped a picture of Franklin holding the finger. "Epic photo," she mumbled.

"Look, you have to delete that," Franklin said, no longer caring if he sounded crazy.

"Why?" the girl asked, pulling the phone in close to her chest.

"Because I look like a maniac. People are going to get the wrong idea. It'll probably turn into one of those internet mimes or something."

The girl rolled her eyes. "You mean memes? Whatevs. I'm totally not deleting it."

Franklin was getting ready to beg her to delete the picture when her phone lit up and she smiled.

"See?" she said. "Josh and Courtney already favorited it. I told you this was a good picture."

"Good for you or good for me?" Franklin asked, starting to panic.

"Who cares about you?" the girl replied. She rolled her eyes, then turned and wandered back out the door, still fidgeting with her phone, though he hadn't even checked the dress in yet.

With Franklin's luck the picture had probably already made it halfway around the world, would be on the cover of every major news website within the hour. The police were probably already looking for him. He could lose his job. Jennifer would keep the

74

girls from him if he got behind on child support again. She'd probably do it anyway, just based on the picture.

He set the finger on the counter and dabbed his forehead with the tainted handkerchief, then dry-heaved when he realized what he'd just done. He picked up the shop's phone and dialed 911.

"I'd like to report a severed finger," he mumbled to the operator.

"A what?" A woman's voice replied.

Franklin dabbed his forehead again, and then tried not to puke, again. "It's kind of hard to explain on the phone," he said in a hoarse, broken tone. "Maybe you could just send over a unit?"

AN ART SHOW
MATING CALL

KATE WAS STANDING IN the center of the gallery discussing the finer points of one of her most experimental pieces when Mandy interrupted her with a nervous look on her face.

"Sorry to disturb you guys, but I need to borrow Kate," Mandy said.

Most of the time such an abrupt interruption would have annoyed Kate, but the disturbed look on Mandy's face had her begging all the necessary pardons and following her friend and yoga instructor past the free-form statues and swirling canvases into the back room of the gallery where they could speak in private.

"So what's up?" Kate asked when they arrived, unable to keep the irritation out of her voice.

"You need to read this," Mandy said, hesitating

for some reason. "But I need you to try to remain calm if you can," she added as she slipped Kate a small, white slip of paper.

"Calm and cent—" Kate started to say, but her mouth fell open as she read the first line of the letter, which had been Xeroxed from a handwritten original. "Oh no … oh god …" she mumbled as she read. "This can't …"

"Okay, okay," Mandy said, failing to hide the panic in her own voice. "It's not that bad. People know what a creep he is, ok? And even if they don't, this isn't exactly a normal thing to do." She took Kate by the shoulders. "Kate, look at me—it's fine," she said.

Kate looked straight through Mandy as her mind worked to provide context to what she'd just read. After a moment she re-focused her eyes. "Where did you get this?" she asked.

"I—promise me you'll stay calm first," Mandy replied.

"Why the fuck do you keep going on about calm?" Kate glared at her. "I'm calm. I'm always calm."

"Kate, you know that's not true. I love you, but remember what happened to my van at Burning Man?"

Kate did remember, though she'd tried to forget.

The Incident, as they now referred to it in her circle of friends, had happened on the third night of the festival. She'd been ass-naked and high on mushrooms while painting a giant psychedelic serpent on a five-foot square canvas as she danced and gyrated to the pulsing beat of a nearby drum circle.

She'd almost lost herself in the experience, entranced by the drumbeat and swirled veins of color until, out of nowhere, *he* appeared, wearing nothing but a pair of brown Carhart pants cut off above the knees to make jorts. He'd slid up behind her, put his hands on her hips and started grinding on her along to the beat.

She' might not have even noticed his hands on her body through the trance if he hadn't dared to slide one up to her breast. The warm feel of his sweaty palm on her nipple had ripped her right out of her trance and destroyed the spiritual energy she'd been working up literally the entire week.

He smelled of body odor and some sour, piney oil. More than anything his unfamiliar scent had made her realize that she didn't know him. She'd shrieked like some sort of wounded animal caught in a trap, causing him to tear his hands away from her body and take a step back.

She'd turned and clawed at his wide eyes with full intention of blinding him. When that had failed, she'd resorted to beating on his chest with her fists as he scrambled to control her wrists.

"You ruined it, you ruined everything, you motherfucker!" she'd bellowed. "Who the fuck are you? What the FUCK do you want from me?"

He'd stumbled backwards, visibly terrified, and tripped over one of the benches they'd brought with them for the campsite, causing him to fall flat on his back just inches from the fire. Kate hadn't wasted any time letting him try to get back up.

She'd grabbed the canvas off her easel, raised it high and impaled it down on his head, splitting it down the middle of the snake she'd painted on it. So that it looked like the snake had just given birth to his face. He'd collapsed on his haunches, dazed, stuck in the canvas like a dog wearing a cone of shame. In a rage by then, Kate had resorted to flipping over benches and boxes around the campsite, then taken to dousing him with some of the open jars of paint, getting it all over the side of Mandy's van in the process.

By the end of her rampage paint was all over everything: the side of the van, Kate's wavy blonde hair, a pile of sleeping bags stacked nearby. She'd had streams of paint running down her sleek, naked body, as had Timothy (she'd only found his name out later).

But all Timothy had done was stand up and take the canvas off his head and bear-hug her from behind over her arms as if it had all been a show of affection. He kept mumbling "I'm sorry" to her over and over again as he pulled her away from the van, which still had paint on it to this day.

Something had changed when she'd felt his warm chest against her back, smelled his piney sweat intermingled with the smell of paint. She'd turned in his arms as if to attack him again and shoved her tongue down his throat instead. They coiled around each other like snakes as she pressed herself into him hard, so hard she knocked him back to the ground, where she dragged his jorts off and climbed on top of him like a cowgirl. When Mandy and the others in their group had shown up from wandering around it was to the sight of them fucking like barn animals next to the fire. After she'd climaxed they'd slept the rest of the night right there butt-naked and covered in paint and sand by the fire.

Timothy had followed her around like a puppy dog the rest of the festival. They'd fucked in inappropriate places like teenagers at a lock-in. When the festival was over and it came time to go back to Austin he'd climbed in the van with her as if it were the most natural thing in the world to do. They'd lived together in her studio apartment since then, with all of the fucking but very little in the way of actual communication.

"Mandy, I'm going to ask you again. *Where* did you get this?" Kate demanded, her mind coming back into the moment again now.

"It's... I... Charlene found it under her windshield wiper out in the parking lot. Apparently he's been putting them on cars and handing them out to anyone that will take one," Mandy said in a meek tone.

"Are you *serious*?" Kate bellowed. Sweat droplets formed in her blond, wavy hair. She took Mandy by the hand without warning and drug her through the crowd toward the front door. People appeared to be staring at them. Kate glared back at them, then opened up the slip of paper and read it again.

To whom it may concern;

If you're attending this art show, then I feel it is my duty to inform you of what you probably already suspect. Kate Williams is a psychotic, self-aggrandizing bitch. Do not under any circumstances purchase any of her vulgar, soulless art. It will almost certainly remain valueless, just as she seems to think that other people's feelings have no value. May she rot in hell, preferably a part that is even hotter than Austin.

--Timothy Briggs, a concerned citizen.

The air outside felt muggy as Kate dragged Mandy out onto the porch. They looked across the dim eastside parking lot to see that every single car in the lot had one of the white slips on its windshield.

Kate leapt down the front porch steps in a fury.

"Kate, what are you going to do?" Mandy called after her.

"Mandy, shut the fuck up and help me," Kate replied. "We have to collect as many of them as we can."

"Kate, it's no use," Mandy started to say, but then she followed behind her instead and began collecting fliers from cars. Kate stomped from car to car as she snatched the slips of paper from under windshield wipers, nearly taking a few of the blades with her when she snatched too aggressively.

She'd collected them off the first row and a half of cars before noticing the shitty red Tercel idling in the back corner of the parking lot, the one that Punk Rock Toby allowed Timothy to use so long as he kept gas in it. He had the driver's side window down and a cigarette's glow hung in the window's void. The thought of him watching her clean up the headache he'd created was more than Kate could handle.

She stuffed the fliers she'd already collected down her pants, having no pockets in her tight grey capris and white spaghetti strap blouse, and broke into a dead sprint toward the red Tercel.

A flurry of motion erupted in the window's frame where the glow of the cigarette had been. The sound of gears grinding filled the air as Timothy tried to shift the car into gear. Kate smiled through her fury, glad she'd refused to loan him the money to replace the worn out clutch on the clunker.

As she closed in on the Tercel, Timothy's head came into view swiveling back and forth between her and the gearshift, that familiar dumbfounded look of panic slathered on his face.

The car didn't cooperate at first. Just as Kate got a hold of the car's window frame the gear clicked into place and the car lurched into motion. She dug her nails into the interior plastic with her right hand and trotted alongside the moving car throwing blind left hooks through the window with her left, though only a few of them connected.

"*Goddammit* Timothy," she said, pummeling him as best she could through the window. "Just what the *fuck* did you think you were doing? You're not going to ruin this for me."

Timothy dodged her punches and attempted to both steer the car away from other cars and roll up the manual window at the same time.

He succeeded in getting the window about three quarters of the way up so that it trapped Kate's right elbow in the remaining space. She had to run to avoid being dragged beside the car after that.

"What did you think was going to happen, motherfucker?" Kate screamed. "Did you think I would just let you get away with this?"

"You shouldn't have kicked me out, I had nowhere to go," Timothy replied, defiance in his voice. He avoided the bumper of an Acura just in time as the Tercel slid out into the street. Kate clawed for his face until he let go of the wheel to protect his eyes.

The car careened straight across the street and t-boned a white Lexus parked in front of the gallery. The impact knocked Kate off her feet and left her dangling from the car window by the arm.

The Lexus's car alarm erupted into action. Timothy shut the Tercell off and dragged himself across to the passenger side. He spilled out the passenger door onto the asphalt as Kate regained her footing and managed to free her arm from the window.

A crowd of people came running out of the gallery to see what the commotion was about. Kate bounded around the car and caught Timothy just as he was moving to flee the scene.

She dove onto his back and put her hooks in like she'd learned in the jiu-jitsu classes she'd taken a year before. She was in the process of rear naked choking him unconscious when someone wrapped their arms around her waist. Kate tried again to claw Timothy's eyes out as several people dragged her backwards now.

She succeeded in digging deep claw marks up both sides of his cheeks with her nails before they pulled her away.

"My eyes!" Timothy sobbed, although Kate had not actually managed to gouge them. "You crazy bitch!"

"My *car*," a male voice called out from the porch behind her. "What the hell happened?"

Mandy appeared and wrapped her arm around Kate's shoulder to lead her past the shocked faces and up the steps toward the gallery's bathroom.

Two men restrained Timothy. His skin-tight capri jorts and striped grey-and-black tank top looked filthy as much from bad hygiene as the scuffle. The owner of the Lexus, a blond man dressed in skinny jeans and a black V-neck shirt, inspected the damage to his car.

At the door Kate turned and looked behind her at the chaotic scene. Timothy sat weeping in the center of the crowd now. His tears intermingled with blood from where she'd scratched him, leaving long pink streaks down his face. Her rage disintegrated at the pitiful, broken sight of him.

She tore away from Mandy's grip and sauntered back through the crowd to Timothy, who was now laid out on the concrete sidewalk sobbing even harder. When he saw her he covered his face as if she were going to strike him.

Instead she pulled his hands away to have a better look at the scratches. They looked nasty. When she reached down her pants the crowd audibly gasped, but she ignored them and pulled out a couple of the fliers she'd stuffed there earlier. She used them to dab the blood and tears from his cheeks.

"*Shhh*," she cooed to him, dabbing at the blood. "*Shhh* …"

"You mangled me," he sniffled.

"I know, I know."

When the police arrived they found them there, tangled like snakes amid a crowd of onlookers, sucking at each other's faces so passionately that some might have thought this had been the point of having the art show all along.

LIFE OF A SALESMAN

BY NOON THAT DAY the sun rose high and just about set the air on fire. I leaned against a pole on the corner of the car dealership's front porch dripping sweat, smoking a butt, and scanning the lot for customers.

A line of cars with colored balloons tied to their windshield wipers faced the service road just off I-35. As I exhaled a cloud of smoke, one balloon slipped loose and floated off into the sky. I have no doubt it eventually landed in just the right spot to suffocate a baby bird or puppy ignorant enough to try and eat it, but that's just the nature of the business, I guess.

I wiped my brow with the back of my hand and a gulf of sweat ran down the side of my head.

Out on the lot, my coworker Jimmy Hernandez was midway through the walk around on a puke-green Dodge Caravan. His customers looked to be a young family.

The woman squinted and smiled from time to time while Jimmy chattered. Every once in a while she rubbed the bump on her belly as if for luck. She held a blond-haired toddler in her right arm with his legs wrapped around her waist like a miniature jiu-jitsu fighter.

Jimmy kept smoothing back his slicked black hair as he spoke, and I couldn't hear what he said but it must've been good, because the woman smiled and nodded a lot, and before long the man was nodding his head and smiling too. When Jimmy used the keyless remote to open the automatic hatch on the back of the van, the husband's eyes lit up like he'd been electrocuted.

It would take a miracle to stop Jimmy from selling those people that van. Or if not the van, something else. Jimmy's entire skillset revolved around an incredible sense of curb qualification. He had a raw instinct for who could buy, and who couldn't buy shit. Once he started talking it almost surprised you that doves didn't fly out of his mouth.

He played the salesman part too, with his greased-back hair and wire-rimmed glasses, acne-scarred cheeks. Jimmy was the only salesman I ever met who wore a suit and tie every day, even in the Texas summer. He'd been selling cars for 15 years and knew every aspect of the business, for better or worse.

"You gotta build the impression of an amazing deal," he told me on my first day. "People love a good show, so the walk around is important, but more than anything else people want to be tricked into believing they can beat the system and get that deal that's supposed to be too good to be true."

Jimmy had his routine down so well that it was

hard to dislike him, even when you knew he'd say or do anything to get what he wanted. He sold the impression of friendship like syrup at a pancake convention. Jimmy put on a hell of a show because he believed in the payoff.

Imagine it: 105 degrees outside and Jimmy out there sweating in that ridiculous suit, gesturing and explaining the benefits of variable valve timing and side impact beams to people who had never bothered to even think about those kinds of details. He looked like the ringleader in a used car circus. Jimmy needed the money, and it showed in his work. Say what you want about the man's lifestyle, but no question he could handle selling under pressure.

By the time I met Jimmy he'd already developed what I would refer to as a substantial cocaine habit. The only thing it never destroyed was his work. When his wife left him, things in his personal life had slipped into a dangerous, out-of-control dimension, but his performance at work never once faltered.

His addiction had progressed threefold in the time I worked with him, so that now he looked gaunt in the face and older than his 45 years. But I swear to God I never once beat the man to work.

A couple of times I saw him twitch or dry heave during the morning sales meetings, but otherwise he handled it almost without effort. Even when rumors circulated among the staff that he'd progressed from the straw to the pipe his performance never suffered.

Our Sales Manager Justin Watts knew all about it, but looked the other way because Jimmy generated a high volume of revenue for the dealership, and none of the carnage ever spilled over into the workplace. When you swim with the sharks you watch your own back, I guess. I don't imagine that anyone was watching Jimmy's at that point. He sure as hell wasn't watching his own.

A rusted Oldsmobile rolled onto the lot and circled through the maze of interior aisles. When it rounded the first corner it came to the area that Justin had us block off with cars to prevent customers from driving straight through.

I frowned. A man who drove a rusted beater probably didn't have the credit or job or income to buy a better one, although he would definitely have the desire. Experienced salesmen didn't waste their time on bogies like these. There's no limit to the amount of your time a determined customer who couldn't finance a loaf of bread will waste trying to, if you let them.

Obvious bogies were reserved for the newer guys like me to practice on. I was the only relatively new salesman on the staff at that point, and even if I hadn't been, I sucked balls at the job, so this type of customer would have fallen to me either way.

The car stopped and parked right in the middle of the aisle. A Mexican man in a button-down flannel shirt, dusted jeans and work boots climbed out squinting against the sun. He wandered over to a black Trans Am on the front line, facing the interstate. I put my left hand in my pocket and walked over to greet him. I pulled a yellow card and a pen out of my front shirt pocket as I approached.

"How you doing today, sir?" I extended my hand to him. He looked at it but didn't move to shake it.

"My name's Marv," I said, pulling my hand back. "I'm a sales associate here. Do you have any questions about this Trans Am I might answer?"

He stared back at me like my prick was hanging out. The look on his face was so convincing that I almost reached down to check, just in case.

"I … no … speak … English. Somebody speak *Espanol*?" he asked.

"*Un momento, por favor.*" I butchered the pronunciation but he shook his head like he understood.

I walked back across the lot into the building, somewhat relieved. I scanned the room, but every other salesperson had a customer. I saw Geoff Wallace easing away from a man wearing sandals with dress socks and a white v-neck t-shirt, so I approached him as he moved toward the back offices.

"Does anybody besides Jimmy speak Spanish?" I asked.

"Nope. I just talked to him at the sales tower and he's got one on the line anyway. Justin just bet him he can't hit a five pounder on that green Caravan. I wouldn't be surprised if the people invite him to dinner tonight after he does it, too."

"I got a customer on the lot that doesn't speak English. What should I do with him?" I asked, trying to steer Geoff back on subject.

"How does he look?" Geoff raised his eyebrows.

"He probably can't buy."

Geoff frowned. "Go tell Justin. Always tell Justin before you let anyone leave. You know that."

I did know that. I didn't want to tell Justin because he liked to fuck with me whenever he got a good opportunity. He'd probably make me go out there and try to sell the guy a car using sign language again. The first time that happened was so bad that I couldn't look anyone in the eye for a week afterwards.

That was when I knew that this wasn't something I could see myself doing in the long term.

I walked to my office in the back and dialed my neighbor Ralph on the phone. I was already planning ways to get hammered as soon as possible after work.

After I finished arranging things with Ralph I started to hang up, but I saw Justin coming toward my office from the showroom right then, so I snatched the receiver back up and pretended to follow up with a customer.

I should mention here that the only thing that pissed Justin off more than a lazy salesman was a lazy salesman who tried to run any amount of game whatsoever on him. You wouldn't try the Jedi Mind trick on Darth Vader. The same concept applied with Justin and bullshit.

"Goddamn it, Marv," he bellowed, "What the hell are you doing back here, you sorry piece of shit?" he was just outside my door then. "The entire lot is fucking full right now. Don't ever let me catch you jerkin' around in your office when there's customers on the lot. You got that? Saturday's the biggest goddamn day of the week."

"Okay," I said.

"Jesus Christ, boy, get busy. There's no way you could be satisfied with what you've made this month. You ain't gonna sell jackshit sitting back here."

I shot up out of my chair and left the phone dangling off the desk. I headed to the showroom with Justin still foaming at the mouth behind me and screaming at one thousand decibels about my ass getting shit-canned pronto if I didn't shape up. I spotted a man in a black baseball cap out on the lot and walked out to greet him.

"Sell him a car, Marv," Justin yelled after me. "Jesus Fucking Christ."

We both knew it wouldn't happen.

* * *

By four I'd taken three more customers but failed to sell to any of them. The first one, a man in cutoff denim shorts and a Mega Death t-shirt, told me to "Go fuck yourself and die." He seriously said it just like that, soon as I walked up, no warning. I got a lung full of exhaust fumes as he sped off in his old rusted clunker. Motherfucker nearly ran over my foot too.

The other two customers approached me before I could get away from them, and I honestly couldn't tell you what they said because I wasn't listening in any kind of meaningful way. I pretended to listen until they stopped talking and then promised to find someone to help them.

Instead I grabbed the keys to a new suburban parked way in the back corner of the lot and headed out there. I climbed in, cranked the air conditioning up to high and took a nap.

By seven, activity on the lot had tapered off to almost nothing. Justin paged the staff to the sales tower. I stood up and went with the others.

"Where's Jimmy Hernandez?" he asked as he slammed the door.

"He's on a test drive with a customer," someone replied.

"Alright then, fuck it. So here's the deal. We had a big day today. Several of you guys got hat tricks. Hell, Jimmy sold *four*, and it sounds like he may not be done yet."

Some of the salesmen whooped at that. Someone

made a comment about Jimmy buying drinks after work. Even if Jimmy had been there that wouldn't have happened, unless by drinks they meant Jimmy would buy an 8 ball of cocaine and a box of baking soda and spend the weekend holed up in some shit-box motel with burned lips and seared fingertips. Justin continued.

"We're slow now, so I'm gonna let a few of you leave early to go chase whores or whatever it is you sleazy sumbitches do at night. Here's what's gonna happen: Anybody who sold a car today can leave right now. By my count, Geoff and Marv are the only ones who don't match up. They stay and watch the lot. The rest of you get the fuck outta here. See you on Monday."

The rest of the sales staff bum-rushed the door and broke out for the employee parking lot in the back. Geoff and I just stood there feeling the effects of the shaft Justin had given us. I went out to the showroom and glanced out the front windows, but the lot was empty. I sat down at one of the chest-high tables in front to keep watch. Geoff came out from the back and took the seat next to me.

"Didn't sell shit either, huh, Marv?" he said.

"Not today."

"Hell, not on most days."

"Okay, not on most days," I said. "But also not today."

Geoff sneered and bounced off to his office like he enjoyed the punishment. Jimmy pulled back onto the lot with two customers in a black Lincoln Town Car. A man with grey hair sat behind the wheel with a focused look engrained on his face, his wife in the passenger seat. Jimmy Hernandez's smiling face poked out between the two from the back seat.

Jimmy motioned the man to pull the car up to the "Sold-line," which was actually anywhere a salesman chose so long as they dropped the word "sold" on the customer.

Justin's sales strategy revolved around forcing the customer to take mental ownership of the vehicle using subtle hints, and to tell the truth it worked pretty well. You might be sitting there right now thinking that psychobabble bullshit wouldn't work on you, but I guarantee you that ten minutes with Jimmy Hernandez doing a walk around on virtually any car on earth would change your life.

Jimmy led the customers inside and seated them at another of the tables on the showroom floor, about twenty feet away from me. Jimmy went into the sales office to talk with Justin, then returned with a smile raked across his face.

"Great news, Mr. Jefferson," he said. "Listen to this! With five-thousand down and a forty-eight month finance term at a 7 percent interest rate I can get you payments of $400 a month on that beautiful Lincoln you just drove. All you gotta do is sign right here and I'll get her cleaned up and ready to go for you."

He indicated a dotted line at the bottom of the worksheet with his eyes and set a pen next to it, then sat back in his chair. The salesman never speaks at this point in the sale. Not until the customer speaks first. This insures that they'll do one of three things. One: Sign the dotted line. Two: Reveal any problems they have with the car or deal. Three: Make serious haste for the nearest exit like the building's on fire.

To tell you the truth, a good salesman doesn't care

which option the customer chooses, and almost no one chooses option one anyway. The idea is to make the customer tip their hand first. Once they start giving up their objections it's much easier to overcome them. The Jeffersons took option number two.

"We told you we were looking to pay $350 a month, Jimmy," the old man said. "This says four. We're on a tight budget—we can't do four. Maybe we're on too much car."

Jimmy didn't even blink before he replied. "So what you're telling me, Mr. Jefferson, is that at three-fifty a month you'd buy this car right now?"

"Wait a minute now Jimmy, just slow down," Mr. Jefferson said, his tone rising. "We may not buy today, like I told you earlier." Jefferson played what he probably thought was his best card, the "I'm just testing the water" card. But no real salesman has ever been stopped that way.

"I understand that, Mr. Jefferson. Not a problem at all. Really right now all I'm trying to do is go in there and get my boss to work with me so we can get you the deal that you're looking for on a car that fits your needs. The Town Car does fit your needs, correct?"

The Jeffersons looked at each other, both nodding their heads.

"Yes, I suppose it does," Mr. Jefferson said, the tone gone from his voice.

"Great, I'm glad to hear it. So my concern then is to find you the best deal possible on that car. To do that I need to know what numbers to get to for you to feel like this is the right deal for you today."

"Today?" Jefferson repeated, as if he were unfamiliar with the concept.

"Yes sir. Today. You see that big rough man in there?" Jimmy gestured toward the sales tower at Justin, who looked a bit like a blonde gorilla dressed in Armani from a distance.

Jefferson nodded.

"He's tired, he's been here since seven this morning. He's ready to go home at this late hour. If I go in there and tell him that you guys only want to see some theoretical numbers on this beautiful car but you don't want to buy it even if you love those numbers, he's gonna stare a hole in me and then tell me that you should come back when you're serious, and we'll discuss options then if the car is still available.

"You noticed that's the only Town Car we have on the lot. That's because a good, dependable car like a Town Car never stays in our inventory for long. To tell you the truth I don't think it will be here much longer, we've only had it for two days. I'll do my best to get you the best deal I possibly can, but we've got to be straight with each other to make it happen the right way."

Mrs. Jefferson spoke for the first time then. "Jimmy, we're not trying to cause you trouble, it's just that we didn't come down here expecting to buy today. We don't want to waste your time."

Jimmy licked his lips. The Jeffersons both sat back.

"That's okay, Trudy, you aren't wasting my time one bit," Jimmy said.

Oddly enough it was true even if she didn't realize that yet.

"But tell me this," Jimmy added, "If I could get you a deal better than you ever expected to see today on this Town Car, better than you thought possible, you would take that deal, wouldn't you?"

"Well, I suppose so." Jefferson grumbled. "Yes."

"Great. So what I need to know is, what numbers would make this become that deal for you, the deal you've been hoping for?"

The Jeffersons eyed each other. Mrs. Jefferson muttered something about interest rates. They came to a consensus in a moment.

"Well, Jimmy, I can tell you right off that we don't have five thousand to put down. And seven percent interest seems a bit higher than we're accustomed to," Mr. Jefferson said.

"Understood. So how much do you have to put down?"

"We thought beforehand that we could come up with two-thousand."

"Great. So what I'm getting is," Jimmy flipped over the worksheet and began to write, "with two-thousand down and ... what interest rate were you hoping for?"

"Five."

"With two-thousand down at a five percent interest rate and a three-fifty per month payment, I will buy this vehicle today."

He pulled the pen from the paper. "Does this look good for you, Mr. Jefferson?"

Jefferson and his wife studied Jimmy's handwriting like it was written backwards, perhaps in Arabic. They nodded their heads, probably out of submission to the indirect pressure more than anything else. "Yes, I suppose so," Jefferson said.

Jimmy drew an X at the bottom of the statement and then drew a horizontal line out from it.

"If I could just get you to initial here, I'll take it to

my boss," he directed.

Jefferson complied. Jimmy hurried off to the sales tower. I shook my head and moved off towards my car in the employee lot.

As I walked past the sales tower Justin shut the door so that he and Jimmy pantomimed through the glass wall as they spoke. I looked back and the Jeffersons seemed pleased with the negotiations.

I should probably mention here that any time you feel like a salesman is doing you a favor, I'd recommend you run like a motherfucker and don't stop until you're at home with the doors locked and the phone off the hook. Just a little friendly advice.

I slipped out the side door to my car, opened a cooler in the back seat and took out two luke-warm beers. I wrapped them in a t-shirt and shut the door, then walked to the far corner of the back lot and ducked behind the concrete wall that hid the dumpsters.

I opened the first beer and chugged half of it before I lit a cigarette. Grey smoke stenciled the humid air when I exhaled it. I finished the first beer and popped open the second. The beers were warm, but I swallowed huge gulps anyway.

There was a hole in the clouds just in front of the moon. It was Saturday night and I wanted to get out on the town, maybe find a lady to try and shack up with. I puffed on the cigarette again. Sweat beaded up on my forehead.

I figured I should get back, but there was no point. I was done with that day. Fuck that, I was done with that job and all the fucking sleazy, soul-sucking bullshit it entailed.

I tossed out my smoke and returned inside to

collect my stuff from my office. Jimmy's customers were just coming out of finance. He pulled around the building in their fresh-washed Town Car. They looked pleased, but I've already talked about what that means.

I snagged my car keys and moved fast back toward the side door. I heard Justin's heavy footsteps stomping down the hall behind me as the side door slammed shut, but I didn't stop or look back.

I closed my car door and started the engine just as the side door to the building swung open. Justin's heavy shape appeared in the framed light. I threw the car in drive and peeled out of the parking spot toward the exit, then turned out onto the service road.

I flipped the headlights on and cranked the radio up. My taillights gleamed red in the rearview mirror as I drove north toward downtown Austin, wondering where a man can find some action on a Saturday night.

QUEEN OF THE ROTTEN

I GOT OFF WORK at the dealership a couple hours later than I expected on account of a deal that went south anyway. I stepped into the club around eleven to the familiar smell of cigarette smoke and aerosol fragrance. The place was about half full and kind of quiet, beyond the stage music. It came off like arriving to a birthday party after the cake has already been served.

I nodded to Hector, the doorman, and he waved me through to a table. Starla, the most recent "I'm-just-here-to-serve-drinks-and-absolutely-not-to-strip" cocktail waitress came over to take my drink order. I guess she didn't realize the rest of them started the same way.

Any strip club regular understands the game the dancers are trying to play. There is no best case scenario, either. Even if you do manage to take one home, you might get stuck paying child support for the next eighteen years, and everything else that comes with that.

Imagine trying to introduce Charlene "The Titty-Twirling-Tap-Dance-Queen" to your son's first grade teacher on parent's night, and then tell me about regrets. You'd think I had more sense than to go anywhere near a scenario like that.

A dancer named Bridget was dry humping the pole up on stage, her maroon nipples bouncing along to the beat. An old man in a beige overcoat leaned against the stage just below her hips, following her every movement with perverted obsession.

Back in the corner the Pyro Twins, Electra and Venus, mingled with a group of rowdy fraternity boys. They almost looked friendly sitting in those strangers' laps and playing with their shirt bottoms just close enough to the crotch to suggest sex. I had to remind myself that Electra had once stolen my wallet, and Venus was a two-time felon.

"Jamison, on the rocks," I told Starla, my eyes glued to Bridget's ass like macaroni to a child's artwork. I settled back into my chair and took in the surroundings: Two Tejanos shooting pool in the corner; a couple of the frat boys off now to see the wizard in the VIP lounge. Helga the Slavic Seductress on deck for the next dance. Finally.

Helga played with her titty tassels as I tried to catch her eye. She pretended not to see me, but I knew she wasn't too good for my money. God knows she'd already had her fair share of it by then. If you could put a price on lust you'd better believe I'd tried.

The first time I saw Helga dance she was dressed

as a Cosmonaut, carrying around a little stuffed space monkey for a prop. She spent most of that night with the space helmet's visor up and a cigarette dangling out of her mouth even when she danced.

I should probably mention that Waldo's Cabaret isn't your standard panties-on, hump-up-the-pole strip club. They're really into themes. I think the theme that night was Space Pussy or something along those lines. Helga looked radiant and ready to blast off straight onto someone's face. I shamelessly hoped it would be mine.

I know I've already pre-qualified myself by saying up front that I know how stupid it is to fall in love with a stripper. And I knew it then, too. To tell you the truth, I don't know why I chose Helga. The fact is most people would have said that Helga was past her prime, if she'd ever had one.

She looked pretty worn, when you got down to it: botox-plastered forehead and ultra-cheap sagging collagen lips. But I liked to imagine what she'd looked like in her younger days, back in Russia or wherever she really came from, before life took to kicking the shit out of her like it does most people.

Like it had done to me. I liked to think of the ways her life might have been different because it kept me from considering my own ridiculous choices, and where they'd led me.

I've been bald since I turned twenty-six. And my bony physique is nothing to clap about. Those are my strong points, really. When I tell people I sell used cars no one ever acts surprised. Maybe that's what I liked about Helga the most. She almost looked worn out enough to put up with a middle-aged failure like myself.

When she took the stage that first night I gave her my full, undivided attention. She snubbed her cigarette out on the bottom of her stiletto heel and mounted the pole like a fucking firefighter.

Man, you should've seen her work it. I was so entranced with the sway in her hips that the astronaut's helmet hit me in the head and knocked me out cold when she tossed it off the stage during her routine.

I woke up on a pile of trash in the alley out back with a massive headache and no wallet. Even still, from that moment on I was hooked. Since then I'd been coming to Waldo's every Tuesday and Thursday night to see her dance. In reality I think that helmet knocked every bit of sense I ever had clean out of my brain.

When Bridget finished her dance, a guy in the corner the dancers called Fat Rob let out a few catcalls by shoving his fingers into the sides of his mouth to whistle. Fat Rob was a regular like me, a loud mouth who always wore a sloppy velour suit and giant gold chain around his neck like some sort of mob movie cliché.

I found myself in constant competition for Helga's attention with Fat Rob. I hated the guy and figured he had to be some kind of phony gangster wannabe, but I never had the guts to tell him so, or to speak to him at all for that matter.

I watched Helga maneuver across the stage with the precision of a woman who knew how to market sex. She took her place with her back to the crowd, her ass cheeks pressed so tight to the pole that it crunched up into her crack.

The first notes of some random eighties love

ballad blasted from the speaker system. Helga slid her ass up and down the pole in rhythm to the beat. Starla returned with my drink and stopped in front of me to set it down. I almost flipped the tray over trying to get her to move out of the way so I could watch Helga dance.

Helga faced the crowd now, bounced her hips and sashayed her arms in front of her face. She walked forward down the runway still sashaying her arms. I moved to greet her at the end. I fished a couple of one-dollar bills out of my pocket to let her know I meant business. Oh, she knew.

When she arrived in front of me she turned her back and leaned her elbows down on her knees, extending her crack toward the sky like a twenty-one-gun salute. Her eyes met mine between her knees. She licked her lips with the tip of her tongue. She worked back up and faced me again, arched one leg forward and indicated I should place the ones in her garter. I slid the bills in.

She withdrew her leg and slid across the stage to the old pervert. He made a sucking sound through his dentures while Helga worked. I told myself that if he were fifteen years younger I'd bash his skull in for ogling her that way, but he'd probably have whipped my ass just the age he was. I'm no tough guy. Besides, we were in a strip club. Really he was just letting her know she was doing her job well.

The geezer slipped some ones into Helga's garter and she moved down the line to Fat Rob. Rob stood in his usual spot as if someone had poured him there. I turned away as Helga worked her maneuvers in front of him, sat down and tossed back my whisky drink. Starla came over and I ordered another round.

"Is that all?" she asked.

I nodded and turned back toward the stage, asking myself why I had such a sweet spot down in the center of my balls for absolutely rotten whores. What was the universe trying to tell me?

Starla returned and set the drink down in front of me, spilling some on my knee in the process. Helga had moved into her second song by then, so I headed back up to the stage to meet her. As soon as she saw me she did some kind of Egyptian titty-shuffle towards me and I thought *Goddamn! What a fucking woman!*

I had such a hard-on I started to worry it might explode through my zipper and point up at her breasts as if to honor them.

Helga hovered over me for a moment, then turned and did her trademark South Dallas Booty Drop so close to my face that my nose almost credit-carded her ass. She must have heard me inhale desperately for a whiff of her scent because she pulled away. Helga was not impressed.

She collected her bills from the floor at her feet this time. She moved down the line to service Fat Rob again.

When the song ended Sasha came up to the stage and replaced Helga. Helga stomped over to the bar where Fat Rob was already waiting to meet her. She leaned in close as if to whisper into his ear. She said something and he smiled, and I thought they both glanced at me, but their eyes shot away when they noticed me watching them.

That made me so nervous I slammed my entire drink on the spot. The whisky felt warm in my chest as the liquor suffocated my anxiety almost before it slid down my throat.

I stood up and moved over to the bar two spots down from Helga and Fat Rob. She lit a cigarette and exhaled a cloud of smoke. The bartender brought her a tumbler of chilled vodka. She knocked it down like water and the bartender filled it again. Helga was way more woman than I could handle, but I had this urge inside me that said I needed to keep trying.

I leaned in her direction and tried to speak as she took the second shot of vodka. All that came out at first was a dull choking sound, so I cleared my throat and tried again.

"Hi Helga, how are ya sweetheart?"

She looked at me like I was some slobbering stalker. I guess by that point I kinda was, but still it hurt to see the disgust in her eyes.

"What you want?" she said, without inflection.

"I—I really enjoyed your performance just then."

Helga studied me as she set down the tumbler. She watched me sweat for a moment in the hostile silence. We had apparently reached some sort of pitiful stalemate.

"How much money you have?" she asked. Fat Rob smiled and started to say something, but he didn't.

"A little. Not a whole lot," I said. It might not have been the best answer, but it was the truth since the deal I spent the whole day working on had fallen through.

"You want private dance? Twenty dollars."

"I'd rather just sit here and have a drink with you, if I could," I said.

Fat Rob snickered and Helga burst into laughter as though she had just learned how. She threw her head back and clutched her bare stomach like it hurt. I thought she'd never stop. The whole room seemed to be watching us then.

"Come back when you have money, little bald man," she said. She sucked on her cigarette again and turned away from me toward Fat Rob.

"I've got a joint in my pocket, we could smoke it out back instead," I blurted out, trying to channel my inner salesman. That seemed to get her attention. She turned to me again and blew her smoke in my face. Her fingers tapped in staggered order on the bar as she considered my proposition. Time did turtle laps through space while I waited for her reply.

"Okay. Follow Helga. Let us go now outside." Her titties bounced as we walked across the club toward the side exit. We pushed through the door and Helga braced a coaster in it to stop the bolt from latching behind us. I pulled the joint in my pocket out.

"Give to me," Helga said as she grabbed the joint from my hand.

She held the lighter to it and began puffing away. I watched as she smoked the first half without offering me so much as a drag. Eventually she passed it without speaking to or looking at me. Scattered garbage and used condoms lined the back alleyway. A few empty beer kegs leaned against the wall.

It felt like a nice night in spite of all that. Just me and an over-the-hill, compulsively abusive stripper sharing a private moment in my delusional mind. When she passed me the joint I even thought that she might be starting to warm up to me, as stupid as that sounds.

Helga wasted no time in shattering that delusion. She grabbed the joint from my hand mid-drag and smoked it aggressively, so that the cherry burned long and hot and orange. It hit her fingers like a wildfire.

"Shit!" she winced. She shook her fingers and tossed the roach out into the night. I wanted to say that I usually tried to save them for later, but no words would come. Helga stuck her finger in her mouth and went back through the door without saying a word. The coaster fell out and the door slammed shut, leaving me alone in the alley with the spent loads and discarded junk.

I tried to open the door to follow her, but it locked from the inside automatically. Motherfucker, I thought. Not again. I walked back around the building and in through the front door. I nodded to Hector as I moved past him. He scrunched his face in return. I sat back down and in seconds Starla had pushed another drink toward me.

"Thanks," I said. I tossed down half of it in the first gulp. The pot started to mingle with the drinks and had me pretty fucked up just then.

I scanned the room for Helga, but she was nowhere in sight. A smoke haze covered the room and reflected the flashes from the strobe light behind Electra on stage.

The strobe and pulsing music started to give me vertigo. By the time the vertigo settled down I had decided to be angry instead. I had the uncontrollable urge to give Helga an ear full. Two months of abuse, apparently that was my limit.

Ten minutes later she stumbled out of the VIP lounge attached to Fat Rob's arm. I stood up and moved towards them like a toddler learning to walk. I found myself standing in front of them sooner than I'd anticipated. Helga licked her lips when she noticed me.

"Listen Helga," I started. "You can't, you can't, you …"

"Hey buddy, relax …" Fat Rob said.

I looked at him up close for the first time then, saw the fat folds of sweaty skin hanging off his neck below that tacky gold necklace, saw the gravy stains on his shirt from the chicken fried steak buffet during happy hour. I'd never hated someone's guts so much in my entire life.

"You! Goddamn—you—fat—slob," was all I managed to say. I'd hoped for something clever, but we take what we can get.

Fat Rob and Helga looked at each other, then erupted into laughter again. Helga's had her arm around Rob's waist with her hand right next to his package. Don't ask me why, but I reached over and slapped it away like I was her fucking grandmother or some shit. I didn't even see the punch that knocked me down.

The world went horizontal and the next thing I felt was Helga's stiletto heel driving down into my chest. She poured her cocktail on my head and spiked the empty plastic glass in my face. Not knowing what else to do, I screamed like a savage then.

I screamed for my loneliness, for death, for all the degrading experiences of a failing, pitiful man, alone in this world. I screamed at the top of my lungs until a size-fourteen penny loafer shut my mouth and ripped my face open.

As the lights faded out around me all I could think was that I would have to find another place to go drinking after work now. If I got lucky they might even have a cleaner alley out back.

NEW ALLEYS FOR NOTHING MEN

TWO PULLED FROM THE WATERS OF LAKE GENEVIEVE

RALSTON LOVED TO HEAR the windows shatter. Sometimes the shot was too far off, or the window didn't break, or he was in a spot with so much traffic he couldn't make out the sound. But it was the times he could hear the sharp crack and cascade of glass toward concrete that brought him the most relief, though the relief was temporary either way.

It was the only thing he'd found that drained some of the venom out of him. If he didn't get some of it out he was afraid he'd do something much bigger, much worse, someday.

And so he shot out car windows with his pellet gun pistol on interstates and at four-way stops, occasionally in truck stop parking lots late at night when he was unable to bum a ride to whatever nowhere town he would end up in next. He'd never really thought of it as a big deal. Just a little tax he placed onto the world for keeping him around, nothing else.

Except this time he had a sense as soon as he heard the glass shatter that everything in the world had just changed. The blue Honda SUV he'd just shot swerved left, slammed off the center median and cut back the other direction like a rock skipped across three lanes of traffic, launched over the guardrail out into the dark space above the lake.

Ralston knew he should run, but his feet wouldn't move. He just stood there gaping at the vacant patch of highway, wondering what kind of madness he'd just brought into the world.

Watching that somersault of lights disappear into the darkness, Ralston finally understood that he didn't really want to hurt anyone at all. The feeling was so powerful that he keeled over and deposited cheap rye whiskey and bile onto the concrete in front of him, then wretched two more times before he could straighten himself up. He needed to do something.

He convinced his legs to move. He heaved the nine-millimeter replica pellet gun out into the water and stumbled his way onto the empty bridge to look off the edge. The drop was maybe fifteen feet at most. The SUV had settled on its side in the water, but the heavier front end was sinking faster than the back, so that now only the driver's side taillight still remained above water.

Ralston's heart hammered in his chest. He thought he might puke again, but it passed. He decided the only thing to do was to go in after it, and his body seemed to toss itself into the water without his mind totally consenting to that choice.

His chest seized up from the cold when he hit the water. His muscles constricted so tight that it was all he could do to doggy paddle in place and gasp in desperation for a deeper breath. The first deep breath came hollow and desperate. Then another. He kicked his legs harder and managed to maneuver himself to the spot where the taillight was just sinking beneath the water's surface. He took a few deep breaths to prepare himself.

The world around him silenced as he dove down into the water, struggling to pull himself deeper to the level of the Honda's driver-side door. He grabbed it by the handle so he could look through the missing window's frame.

Inside, the female driver was turned around with her shoulders between the two front seats, her butt in the air. He pulled on the door handle and it gave with a lurch.

He thought the woman might be dead until she turned and gave him a terrified look, her face glowing in the red light from the car's instruments. Ralston was amazed she had any air left in her lungs.

He didn't have time to consider the options. He just wrapped his arms around her waist and begun dragging her back out the open door. The car had started to really sink now. The woman thrashed her arms as if trying to get away from him. Ralston held on tight with his right arm and used his left to pull them both out of the car. She clawed his arm and he almost let go, but didn't.

She thrashed and screamed all the air out of her lungs. Ralston summoned the last bit of strength left in his body and heaved her out of the car as her body went limp in his arms. He fought back the urge to suck in water himself. It felt like the world was sinking away. With his last bit of strength he kicked his feet toward the surface and lost consciousness.

* * *

Ralston came to on his back with an old man's face hovering just above his own, preparing to blow into his mouth. He spit up water and choked and gagged, curled up into a ball on his side.

"Easy there," the man said. "Just relax, you've been in an accident."

Ralston coughed some more as liquid came out of his nose. He let the man ease him onto his back, until he remembered where he was and sat straight up.

"Easy," the man said again. "It's alright, just relax."

"Where is she?" Ralston whispered, trying to look around through blurry eyes.

"She's okay, just relax. Do you remember what happened?"

Everything came back to him then. He cocked his head and puked up some more water. The man covered his nose and leaned back. "Smells like you've had some liquor tonight. Were you driving?"

Ralston cleared his throat and took a deep breath. It was hard to speak. "No," he said. "I saw her go in the water. She hit the median and then went off the other side into the lake. I went in after her."

The old man nodded and patted him on the shoulder. "You did good, son," he said. "She's alive. You're a hero."

The word *hero* echoed in Ralston's mind. Hero.

He was nothing but a goddamn drunk. Almost a killer, too. That got him to shaking.

"I've got some towels up front," the old man said. "I'd best grab 'em before you go into shock. We saw her go off too. Lucky we were on our way back from doing a little night fishing, else I don't know what would've happened to you two. Earl over there pulled you out of the water."

Ralston's eyes adjusted and he could see that he was on some sort of fishing boat. The old man moved off to get the towels.

Two men were attending to the woman on the other side of the boat. From the look on her face she must have been in shock. She kept mumbling something to herself but Ralston couldn't hear the words, could only see her mouth moving.

The men were dressed in clear rain ponchos even though it wasn't raining. One of them, a middle-aged black man who must have been Earl, had tears running down his cheeks. Maybe he knew the woman, or maybe he'd just been scared.

The old man stopped as he passed them and Earl said something to him. He nodded. When he made it back to Ralston his face had gone slack.

"What is it?" Ralston asked him. The old man looked at his feet and extended a towel out to Ralston, who took it with a shaking hand. "What happened?" he asked again. The old man met his eyes then.

"I don't really know how to say it," he began. "It's …" he trailed off, put his palm to his forehead as if it might help him speak. It did.

"She … there … there was a child in the car. An infant." He spit those last two words out like they tasted sour. "Oh dear God," he added, dropping his face into his hands.

Every hair on Ralston's body stood on end. He retreated into his thoughts then, forced to revisit the one place in time that he was always trying to drown out. Forced to remember the last time he'd stomped out a child's life.

He remembered the look on Charlene's face when she came out of the clinic that day five years ago. It was like he could see the love drain right out of her eyes when she looked at him in that moment. Maybe she'd never loved him. If so it wasn't her fault.

He hadn't wanted to be a father, not until it was too late. It was the last time he could remember that she'd ever looked at him at all. Afterwards she just looked through him as if he didn't exist. Now, in this moment, he wished that he didn't. He wished he could take back every single thing he'd ever done in his life, erase it all from existence like hanging up a phone.

"I don't understand," he said to the old man, just as he'd said the day Charlene told him she was leaving. But he had understood then, just as he understood now.

The old man put his hand on Ralston's shoulder again and shook him back into the moment. "You did what you could," he said. "You saved her life. Nothing you could have done for the child. You're still a hero."

Ralston shook his head. He wished more than anything that were the truth, but he could already feel himself drowning in the lie.

MIDNIGHT AT THE SAN FRANCISCAN

THE MOMENT THEY LET me out of the state penitentiary up in Santa Fe I set off straight away to do this. I'd made my mind up about it years before. In fact, if I told you it had become my sole purpose for living, that would still be an understatement. Nothing — not time, perspective, forgiveness — nothing could have stopped it from happening.

That I would surrender my life was a given, is a given, you might say. Because sitting here eating my last rib eye in this gaudy red vinyl booth, the same booth Marie, Ava and I used to sit in ten years ago every Friday night for our family dinner together, my resolve has never been stronger.

It feels good to know the moment has almost arrived, that soon I'll be able to leave this life with the scales as balanced as they're ever going to get, even if that could never be enough.

Perhaps I should explain. My name is Mike Treadwell. I used to be a family man, an upstanding member of this community. I owned an auto garage, just south of here out on Highway 70, that did mechanical and minor body work. I was a good father. A good son, too, however unnoticed that went. I was the kind of neighbor who might mow your yard for you while you're at work, the kind of man who always did the right thing as I saw it.

There was a time I could walk down these streets and people would wave, say "Whadaya say there, Mike, how's the wife?" or "I'll be in next week, Mike, the farm truck needs another tune up." There was a time when things still mattered to me that weren't trapped in a time already passed. To tell you how I fell so far, I'll have to start at the beginning. So that's where I'm going to start.

I grew up in Reno, the only son of a man who never wanted daughters, but got two of them anyhow, along with me. When he wasn't driving me toward the lost achievements of his childhood, my father dealt blackjack over at Harrah's. My mother was a cocktail waitress there too, though that's not how they met. No need to go back that far anyway.

They worked overnights, which meant that from the time I was ten I was responsible for my two sisters — getting them dressed and feeding them breakfast, getting them to the bus on time, that kind of thing. I loved my sisters, though my father's default mode was to ignore them. He'd wanted more sons, not daughters. It never should have surprised him what a tragedy their lives became, and I don't think it would have surprised him to see what a tragedy mine became either, had he lived long enough.

At nineteen I met a girl, my Marie, and we moved here to Las Cruces together for a job she found working as a secretary. The job didn't last but we stayed anyway, mostly because we didn't have the money to move back. Within a few years we had a child together, Ava. The first time I saw her something snapped into place inside me, and all my aggression just melted away. I felt such joy when I found out she was a girl that I cried for the first time in fifteen years. I vowed never to treat her with the same neglect my father had shown my sisters, for no other reason than because they had no interest in hitting a baseball or throwing around the pigskin. I had seen firsthand what neglect can do to a person's soul, and I swore that would never be Ava.

For the most part my father just whipped my ass every time I failed to secure the starting position or missed the cut for varsity football, so maybe they were lucky in some ways. But the one thing my father did pass on to me was a deep knowledge of how to fix cars, which I think maybe his father had taught to him, though he never said that. And it served me well that he gave me that one thing, even if his trying to teach me led to an ass-beating most of the time.

But anyway, by the time Ava was born I'd already left that life behind and taken over the garage here in Las Cruces. Marie and I had gotten married the year before and started trying to have a kid right away, though it took a while.

Ava was my little blue-eyed princess. Marie used to bring her by the garage every day after school, and God did I love to see that smiling little face appear in the window of my office. She always waited to be beckoned inside before she would open the door and jump into my arms to tell me "I love you more than the ocean is deep, daddy." To which I'd reply "I love you more than the sky is high," and she'd laugh and nuzzle her face into my dirty work shirt while I smiled at Marie over her shoulder.

You don't understand what real love is until you have a child of your own. You can love other people for who they are, what they do, anything, really, but it's not the same. You love your child the way that you love yourself. More than you love yourself, in fact. They're like a chance to start over and correct the hard or miserable things inside you. It's as if everything that gave you value in this world has gone straight into them. They become your treasure, your hopes and dreams for the future. There was nothing I wouldn't do to protect my Ava. Nothing.

So things went along as they do. Years passed by turning a wrench underneath cars, and Ava got taller, smarter. And sweeter. She was my best friend, funny as that sounds. Children have so much wisdom wrapped up in their innocence. Ava healed me, kept me from thinking about all the things I'd left behind me that I never talked about to anyone, that are still hard for me to talk about even now.

Marie and I loved each other so much back then too. I regret spending so much time working. I thought I was doing the right thing for my family. Now I see it was all a sham, a lie the world found a way to make me believe. Today I'd trade every dollar I ever earned for thirty seconds with those two girls, but it's too late. That's the way life works. You never understand anything until it's too late to fix it.

And then Ava got sick. We didn't understand

what was going on at first; she just kept getting dizzy, sometimes throwing up from it. Marie shuffled her back and forth from the doctor, poor Ava sometimes vomiting in the back seat of the car, having the worst vertigo I've ever seen a child have. I'm telling you it absolutely killed me inside to see that. Every single time it happened I begged the universe to do it to me instead, but that's not how it works.

At first the doctors couldn't figure out why she was so dizzy, so sick. They ran tests on her as we ran up the credit cards trying to pay for it all without health insurance. We were barely getting by before on what I took home from the garage, so you can imagine we were soon swept away in a sea of debt. But none of that mattered to me or to Marie. We just couldn't stand to watch that sweet child suffer so much. We needed answers, and that took money.

I'm not proud of what I did. I told Judge Dalton Freeberg the same thing, but he just stared right through me as if he couldn't understand the words. But I don't blame him; he was just doing his duty, like I had been doing mine for Ava. He could have given me far more time if he wanted to, not that it would have mattered at that point.

The waitress, Charlene, is hovering over my booth now. "Can I get you anything else?" she asks. "The kitchen is closing and I'd like to start sorting out my tickets and such."

"One more Manhattan and the check," I say, giving her as much cheer as any man with a .38 special and two full .380s tucked into his trench coat can. I didn't bring any extra clips or ammo. I'm not planning on needing to reload.

Charlene makes off for the kitchen. She doesn't

remember me, or else she doesn't recognize me beneath this beard. She waited on me and Marie once a week for years, but that was over ten years ago now. She looks every bit of ten years' older too. Waiting tables will do that to you, I guess. I can't imagine how much older I must look, but I don't care how anyone sees me anymore. I've already been dead for ten years in all the ways that matter. If I look it, that's fine.

Charlene returns with the Manhattan and the check tucked into one of those black pads restaurants use, then she's gone again, probably to do her busy work so she can get off shift. I tuck a hundred dollar bill into the pad and shut it. The tables around me have emptied now. I'm the only one in the room. Karaoke drifts from the doorway that leads back into the bar area.

The drinks are good at The San Franciscan, and so is everything else. Used to be I could have smoked a cigarette right here at the table, but the whole world changed while I was in prison. Now you can barely smoke on your back porch without someone laying into you from across the fence.

But you don't need to hear about any of that. Back to what I was saying. Judge Freeberg, he gave me nine years, and though he could have given more, I still hated that he couldn't take the reason I did what I'd done more into consideration. Not that I could have saved Ava then anyway, but you can bet your ass I would have kept trying.

They call it "a war on drugs," but that's not what it really is. It's a war on poor people. It's a way to keep the desperate folks from climbing out of the gutter and standing tall in this world. The only thing upwardly mobile in America is the money itself, which always ends up at the top, while the rest of us starve and watch our children choke and cry and suffer because there's no money to make the people who can help them richer.

I said "Fuck that." Not my Ava. When we found out it was a brain tumor, there was no way I was going to just let her rot away over money. The garage was already mortgaged to the hilt, and we'd never set enough money aside to come close to buying a place of our own. The only thing I had to sell was my ability to do good body and mechanical work. When my employee Raul came in one day and said "Mr. Mike, you still wanting to make more monies?" I didn't even blink.

"Of course," I told him.

"Even illegal stuff, even if it's drogas?"

"If it pays right, I'll do whatever it takes," I said.

"My friend, Cesar, his guy looking to have work done on some cars, secret places in the body can be fill with coca, mota, things like that. He want to have them pack and weld into the cars, so that the policia cannot easily find them. I tell him about your problems, he say maybe you can help each others out?"

"What's the pay?"

"He no say. I only tell him I ask you to meet him, he say okay."

"Okay," I said, already knowing I was getting myself into things I had no business getting into. "So let's meet him."

For the record, Marie was against the whole thing, right from the start.

"Drugs, Mike, really?" she said. "Have you lost your mind? Those guys are probably in a cartel. They could be dangerous. I won't stand for you putting this family in that kind of danger. We can figure something else out."

"Figure what else out?" I asked her, not waiting for a response before I added, "She could die, Marie. Worse, she's in pain. I don't know how much longer I can watch her be in that kind of pain, you know?"

"I do," Maria said. "Baby really you know I understand, but this thing you're proposing, there'll be consequences, I can feel it."

"She's going to die if we don't get her help. Can you feel that?"

"Don't mock me," Marie snapped. "You always do this. I trust my instincts, Mike. It's up to you if you want to trust yours. I can't help it if the whole idea of this repulses me to the core."

That backed me up a little, though not enough to abandon the idea. "I don't know what else to do," I said after a minute, "It repulses me too, but not as much as the thought of that sweet little girl in the other room having to lay around sick and dizzy and dying for however long it takes to finally get dead."

That seemed to get through to her.

She said: "Then do what you feel you have to do, Mike. But protect us. I don't want this coming back on our family. Make damn sure nothing can come back to us."

"I'll do my best," I said.

"That's not good enough. Do better," she said, and I should have known then just how much was really at stake. That is, everything. I would have changed courses, done something else, whatever that would have been, had I realized how it would go. But at the time I figured the less she knew the less implicated she would be if something went down, so we never talked about it again.

We loved each other. Even through all the stress with Ava being sick and money running short, I'm telling you that we were always in love, always committed to each other. When I married Marie I meant it to be for the rest of my life.

So Raul brought Cesar and his guy into the shop the next afternoon. At the time I didn't know the man's name, I just knew that he had dead eyes, that he only spoke to me through Cesar as a translator, and that within an hour of him stepping foot in my shop he had me hooked into a business that would come to destroy my life in short order.

I found out from Raul later that his name was Felipe Delgado, though to most people in his business he was known as El Frio. The Cold One. He'd gotten the nickname from his ability to perform atrocious tasks, things that average men would shudder and shy away from, without blinking an eye.

The scariest thing about him was that beyond his blank eyes he looked like any normal migrant worker you might see on the streets — faded and dust-stained jeans under a plaid pearl snap, an old straw cowboy hat that looked like it had never existed ten feet away from manual labor at any given moment. He had a moustache that made him look more like someone's quirky father than a drug trafficker. That man could have sat next to you on a bus and you'd have no idea what kind of evil was inside him unless he lifted the brim of his hat so that you could see his eyes.

The arrangement with El Frio required me to install a special gas tank into two vehicles each week, a tank that could only be accessed by taking the car apart, and had a built-in barrier that split the tank size in half but could fit five kilos of cocaine in the extra compartment. The tanks had some sort of lead-based paint coating on them that made them heavy as hell, but I guess made it tougher to x-ray them or something.

I assumed the cocaine was coming out of Juarez via El Paso, but didn't know for sure back then. I never asked where the vehicles were going, but I can tell you that the way we sealed the tanks up, they had to cut them back open on the other end, which must have been dangerous. It was a pretty clever configuration, not foolproof, but any cop sniffing around there would have to go to a lot of trouble to find the stash, even if the cars did probably have to stop twice as often for gas.

But anyhow the money helped, and we were able to get Ava booked for surgery to remove her tumor. The doctors told us it was a long shot, and even if it worked we were going to need to do chemo, too. About a month in, I realized that even with the work for El Frio it wasn't going to be nearly enough money, so I asked Raul to see if he had more work.

"I check and see," he said. "But be careful, Mr. Mike. People, they start out casual, but this thing, it will suck you in so deep you can never climb back out. Is what happened to Cesar."

I told him I understood, but this was the way it had to be. I was operating on the assumption that once Ava was better I would figure a way to get out, which, if anything, speaks to my naiveté and desperation as much as anything else back then.

But El Frio didn't have any more work for me, as it turned out. In fact he explicitly forbade me from doing anything more than I was doing. He wanted to keep my garage as insulated from heat as possible.

Still, I needed money ASAP, damn everything else. It didn't take me long to figure maybe they weren't the only folks in town who might have a use for a secret compartment installed into their vehicle. I didn't have the gas tanks with the lead coating, but I did have a few other tricks up my sleeve.

I had Raul put out the word that I was open to doing "creative" body work, similar to what I'd been doing for El Frio, and before long he brought me a couple of hippies named Teddy and Nicholas who wanted me to retrofit the spare tire on a Toyota 4Runner to look normal even when filled with several pounds of vacuum-sealed marijuana. Then it was a man named Willets, who wanted a stash compartment behind his radio, accessible through a false wall inside the glove box. In no time at all, I was doing ten or twelve such installations a week, and the extra money, though still not enough, put us on the path to saving Ava's life, I felt.

Except I was suffering from a shortsightedness that has been torturing me ever since. Though what I was doing by installing these stash spots in cars was not technically illegal, it had a lot of potential to bring heat. It was only a matter of time until one of those low-level drug dealers got popped and sucked me in to their arch around the toilet bowl. And that's exactly what happened.

I heard all these details later on, mind you, while examining the case documents with my attorney. What happened is that I installed a tiny compartment on a Subaru Forrester for a teenager named Steven Cain that allowed him to stash his weed in the car without his parents finding it. Or at least, that's what he told the police he'd wanted it for. I never asked him for a reason.

But when a Ventura County sheriff's deputy pulled him out of the Forrester for DUI one night, Steven hadn't closed the compartment properly in his haste to stash a quarter gram of cocaine in it. The deputy found his stash, and they hadn't even made it to the station before Steven was insisting he knew someone involved with all the drug dealers, someone who had to be knee deep in drug sales. That someone was me, and though he was full of shit, it turned out he was right in one very important way. The gas tanks.

Ava had gotten her surgery by then, and she was recovering really well in the hospital, though they were on me almost constantly about money. She looked pitiful with all her curly brown hair shaved off and her head wrapped in bandages. It took two days before she woke up, and it was the most scared I've ever been in my life.

I don't know if the hospital didn't want to know or didn't care where I was coming up with so much cash, but I've never met a man yet who had much compunction about taking cash once you put it in their hand. Least of all a doctor or hospital administrator. So long as they kept taking it I could have cared less, I just wanted to be there to sing "You Are My Sunshine" to Ava when she was feeling bad.

Like a fool, I was starting to believe at that point that everything could work out, that I'd be able to get out of all this nefarious activity within a year or two and my family could go on living in peace. That Ava would grow up and get married, and have a daughter of her own to love. She had the kindest heart I've ever encountered. I'm not just saying that, either. One smile from her would have cheered a man at the gallows. She could sense when I was stressed, and she'd climb up into my lap and give me butterfly kisses that made it all fade off into the distance. In fact it happened the very morning my life fell apart.

That night Raul and I were sitting side-by-side, taking a break before installing one of the lead-painted gas tanks, when the S.W.A.T. team kicked in the garage's front door. A spewing tear gas canister hit the floor at our feet, and more men with guns than I've ever seen in my life rolled in screaming at us to get on the ground, pointing AR-15s and pistols with red laser beams in our faces. Which, of course, we did.

Charlene is at the edge of the table again now.

"Here's your change," she says.

"Keep it," I reply.

She hesitates, as if worried there are strings attached to the money. "Are you sure?" she finally asks.

"I'm sure. Sorry for keeping you so long."

"Well thank you. And it's not a big deal. But if you could, would you mind moving into the bar room? I mean, if you're gonna stay? I've got to close down this area of the dining room before I get off shift," she says.

I nod. I can't blame her, she's probably had a long day, wants to go home to her children, if they're still at home. I nod without responding to her and slide across what feels like a mile of red vinyl out of the booth. In another life I'd put a booth like this in my kitchen and not give a damn if people thought it was crazy. I'd sit in it with Ava and Marie and love the world away over breakfast every morning.

But you only get one life, and mine is almost over. No use thinking about things like that. The clock is still ticking, and I've got more to tell you.

Anyway, they hauled us off to the station, along with the five kilos of cocaine in the gas tank. I kept hearing Marie's voice telling me about her bad feeling.

At the station they leaned on us every which way you can lean on a man. I spent twelve hours with a light in my face and an asshole narcotics officer blowing smoke from his Kool cigarettes at me without even offering me one. They had no idea where the cocaine had come from. They just knew that a guy like me, no way he showed up with it on his own accord.

I didn't say a word. Not one peep. Even when the man told me he could get me out of everything, I wouldn't budge. A man doesn't get a name like El Frio from a drug cartel for being understanding. They shuffled me through courtrooms and stuck me with a court-appointed attorney who knew about as much about defending a man in my position as I know about quantum physics. He tried to turn my defense into a one-man crusade against the drug war and mandatory minimum sentencing—I guess because there's not much you can do when the law says a fella has got to do a certain amount of time either way.

In the meantime the money ran out and Ava wasn't getting her chemo. I cried and beat my arms bloody against the cell walls when I found that out, but if it mattered to anyone they didn't show it.

The last time I saw my daughter it was through two-inch-thick shatterproof glass, and she looked so pale that I almost fainted on the spot. Even then she managed to give me a weak smile, but it only served to bury my heart. The last thing she ever said to me was "I miss you daddy, come home soon," and I realized that even though she was dying, she was still worrying about me.

When the visit was over I had to be carried back to my cell. They didn't even do me the dignity of allowing me to hold her, to touch her one last time. I begged the guard, asked him if he had children, but I was already a number to him, nothing worth risking his job over.

The next time Marie came to see me Ava wasn't with her.

"I have to tell you something, Mike," she said. I already knew what she was going to say. Nothing else could have made Marie look like that. Nothing. I sat up straight and balanced my hands on my knees as if to brace for it.

"Ava's back in the hospital. The cancer has spread to her lymph nodes and kidneys," she said, tears streaming down her cheeks. "I don't think she's going to make it, Mike, maybe not even another week or two."

My blood ran cold and reality seemed to toss me out on my ass in that moment. It felt like I was looking down on everything. All I could see was the shatterproof barrier that stood between us. She said something else so soft I couldn't hear it over the ringing in my ears.

"What?" I said.

"I said you should be here with us, Mike, not in there. You should have trusted me. This is your fault, Mike. You messed up and now our daughter is going to die."

My face burned and my hands shook. If reality

had kicked me out a moment before, it hammered me back into my body then, though all I felt with it was profound pain. I couldn't argue with her, couldn't tell her I was sorry or ashamed or that I loved her. She seemed so far from me that I felt guilty even saying her name.

I don't remember if she said goodbye or not. I barely remember the guards hoisting me up between them and dumping me back in my cell. I stopped eating or drinking until the doctor at the jail said I would die in a day or so if it continued, so they got a court order and put a feeding tube in my belly. I didn't try to stop them. Matter of fact, I didn't do anything at all.

When I woke up in the jail's infirmary, it was to absolute misery and suffering. I had never felt so alone in my entire life, not even when my father was beating the snot out of me and everyone I'd ever known looked the other way like it wasn't happening. I thought it was impossible to suffer any more than that, which turned out to be another mistake, because the day they told me my daughter was dead I realized I'd only been standing at misery's door. I'd not yet even stepped inside.

And still that wasn't the bottom. The amazing thing about human beings is that we can suffer and survive through just about anything. The God that made us either loved us so much that he made us damn near unbreakable, or hated us so much he made us to withstand unfathomable suffering. Either way we seem to survive through things you wouldn't think a cockroach or a crocodile could make it through.

Marie stopped coming to see me after that. The

State Corrections Department moved me up to the Santa Fe unit and I never saw her again. To this day I don't know what was in her heart afterwards. For sure grief for our daughter, but I couldn't tell you if she loved me or hated me the moment that some gun thug working for El Frio put a bullet between her eyes to pay me back for taking on shady work after he'd forbidden it.

I found out from the prison chaplain, a man named Randy Ford. I've never been religious, but he was a good man, and in his own way as comforting as a man can be when he's tapping the final nail into your coffin. Marie had been executed at pointblank range. Her murder was never solved, though a fool could see who'd done it. Up to that point I'd been afraid he would come after me in prison, that's how self-absorbed I'd become.

It wasn't until Marie was murdered that I realized his punishment for me was to have me sit by, powerless, while he murdered my wife, and then have me live with that knowledge—a walking example of what happens when you step on El Frio's toes. If I even thought of selling him out, I'd never have made it through lunch the next day, so he wasn't worried about that.

What I don't think he counted on was my ability to survive such horrors. If he'd understood how much I loved my family, he would have killed me for sure. Never underestimate your enemy, nor his ability to pull years of breath out of nothing but the will to see you destroyed.

The restaurant's bar area is starting to fill up for karaoke. A couple of middle-aged drunks are finishing up a Journey tune I can't remember the name for anymore. I grab a seat at the corner of the bar, where I'm hard to see from the entrance but still have a clear view of the action up on stage. Mirasol Delgado and her friends should be arriving any minute for her weekly karaoke session.

That's another thing that happened while I was in prison. Everyone thinks they're a pop star now, so someone rounded a bunch of them up and put 'em on television. There was a time when music meant something, now it's just about being famous. You can bet your ass I won't miss that when this is over.

I've heard Mirasol sing before, though, and she's not bad. I've seen Mirasol do a lot of things, because I've been following her, learning every intimate detail of her routines. You see, my old friend El Frio took up residence south of the border not long after I got busted. He's become a right bit more famous in the time I've been away, and risen a few pay grades in the process. He's become some sort of boss for the Juarez Cartel, and probably even Mirasol doesn't know how to find him on a given day.

I order a beer now instead of another Manhattan. I need to keep my head somewhat straight. It's 11:00, the guest of honor will arrive any minute for her half hour in the spotlight. I pay cash for the beer and sit back to nurse it while a couple of college girls absolutely massacre some obscure pop song on stage. Or maybe that's just how the song sounds. It's hard for me to tell anymore.

Mirasol and her two girlfriends Tati and Flora walk through the door at 11:10. The three men who enter behind them could be mistaken as their dates to the casual eye, but in fact they're bodyguards under the employ of El Frio himself.

I guess I don't have to point out that one of the things that makes these drug cartels so much scarier than other forms of organized crime is their complete disregard for any kind of code. They go after family the way a wolf goes after the weakest member of a herd. It's pure predatory instinct, the kind you can only build in a person by spending years grinding them into the gutter first. Well, I've done my years, so here I am.

Mirasol shows no signs of any such upbringing. She's probably had guards most of her life. A fool could see she's had it pretty easy compared to the way her father was probably raised. That is, until now.

The other two girls manage to snag a booth and slide into it as Mirasol goes straight to the DJ's table and signs up to sing. I can tell you from experience that, while she could sing a host of various new pop songs, my money is on anything by Selena. There's nothing special about Mirasol's voice, but you can tell she really feels the music, that it means something to her. It's the kind of hard won meaning each of us earns to varying degrees after having life kick the shit out of us once or twice. The variance can be accounted for only in the level of violence the world brings against us, but almost all of us have it somewhere inside us, excepting men like El Frio. In a perfect world it might have saved Mirasol's life, because her eyes could not be farther from the blank soullessness of her father's when she sings.

I learned a lot in prison about the human need for meaning, the need for purpose and connection to keep us putting one foot in front of the other. The first couple years after Marie and Ava were gone I collapsed in on myself. I swear to God it didn't matter to me one bit that I was in prison. I would've felt the same way if you put me in The Penthouse Suite at The Playboy Mansion.

It took me a while to whittle and shape my grief into purpose, and only when I found that sense of purpose did it matter to me that I was locked up. Not because those walls stood between me and the outside world, but because they stood between me and my very last purpose on this planet. Just now my purpose is taking the stage to sing, totally unaware of her impending date with destiny.

Mirasol cups the microphone in her hand and pulls it from the stand with the confidence of an experienced performer. When she starts to sing the whole room perks up to listen. And she's on tonight, no doubt about it. I can't understand the Spanish words that come from her lips, but they feel familiar from the soul she puts into them. Her green eyes flash and flare in the house lights. She twirls and shimmies in that graceful affect of young men and women who do not yet realize they can become old.

Even her guards are taken by her stage presence. Especially the one with the goatee, who's on his third beer already, and seems to have no idea that anyone would even have a reason to keep track of that. Mirasol's song ends and everyone applauds. She smiles and replaces the mic, then takes up her spot with her friends. She's replaced by an old man in a brown leather coat he must have gotten when he was still in high school, trying to sing a Frank Sinatra tune that I cannot remember the name to, any more than he can remember the words.

If Mirasol stays true to habit she'll sing one more song, and be gone by midnight to some Latin dance club or college-kid hot spot her friends want to go to tonight. All on Mirasol's dime as far as I've been able to tell. But money wouldn't be money if it didn't bring some leeches along with it.

I count six going on seven Coronas now between her guards. If they stay true to habit they'll have had eight before we leave, five for the one with the bald head and three for the one with the goatee. The one in the car who drives them around never drinks, but he'll be too far away once the action starts to do much. I'm feeling pretty goddamn drunk myself, but I've got surprise on my side.

A few more decrepit singers make their way across the stage, along with a redheaded woman who isn't half bad, was probably something to look at fifteen years ago. Now she just looks like she drinks, which I can tell you is true because she's been here every single time I've come in while following Mirasol.

If I had to pick one thing that prison made me good at, it's patience. Before I went in I didn't have an ounce of patience, but all those years plotting and imagining gave me an uncanny ability to take my time about things, to wait for the right moment and always plan for variables. If I'd had those things when I was younger I'd never have gone near a guy like El Frio. Maybe my family would still be alive, or maybe not. One of the tricks to learning patience is to never let your mind slip to the time that has already passed. Always stay focused on your purpose. Everything else is just a distraction. This, the lights, the guards, all of it is a distraction. I only need to wait a little while to avoid it. Besides, even El Frio's daughter deserves the opportunity to sing one last song.

She takes the stage again to a half-hearted applause. As the first notes sound from the speakers, every hair on my body stands on end. It's the last thing I ever would have expected a girl like Mirasol to sing, and it's like having someone reach into my chest and squeeze my heart as hard as they can. It was Marie's favorite song.

"Your love," Mirasol coos, her slight accent strangely fitting, "is lifting me higher, than I've ever, been lifted before ..."

My God, did Marie love Jackie Wilson. I can't imagine there are many people who don't. The entire room is transfixed; people are nodding their heads now and swaying back and forth. And Mirasol, she looks like a legitimate star up there, shaking her hips, closing her eyes for the chorus as a couple people whistle and others sing along. My heart thumps. My eyes water. My anger is welling up, but it's not alone. Everything shifts in and out of focus. I've had too much to drink.

Mirasol is giving the show of her life up there. Maybe it's because the song itself is so powerful. Everyone cheers as she hits the climax. I can still see Marie dancing around our kitchen and singing the same song while Ava claps and laughs.

The song ends and the room erupts into applause. I drop a twenty on the bar and maneuver my way closer to the front door. Mirasol moves back to her table. I stay back in the shadows, just another workingman minding his business as he drinks off the day's work. The time has come.

Mirasol wades through the crowd to the bar and drops money in front of the guards, meaning they're ready to go. I lean on the wall, my hand shaking on the .38 inside my coat as they stand up and collect their things for the road. I'd planned to be calm for this, not so drunk and shaken up. I can't remember the last time I let myself feel anything, and it's already sucking the life out of me. The only way to deal with the kind of pain I've been through is to lock it in the deepest part of your soul, and that means locking anger in there with it.

A blast of cool air hits me as the goateed guard opens the door for Mirasol and company to step out onto the sidewalk. When they've all gone out I wait until he drops the door to catch it and head out behind them.

Just another night in the desert, air that's cool and clear and empty. A few cars make their way down the street. Mirasol and her friends have already rounded the building's corner moving toward the parking lot, the two guards right behind them. My focus blurs in and out from the booze. I take four long, fast strides toward them and shoot the one without the goatee in the back of the head.

Everything descends into chaos then.

Screams erupt. Heels click against asphalt as I shift the .38 and try to pop the other one, but he flinches from the first shot and the second goes right by his face. He drops to a knee and turns fumbling with his pistol. He gets off one half-aimed shot before I unload the last four bullets from the .38 into his chest. He makes as if to shoot at me again, but his hand never comes back up; he just stares at me in terrified shock.

Mirasol and her friends are only ten feet from the big black Suburban her father's men drive her around in. I drop the .38 and pull out the two .380 Berettas. I've never tried to shoot two pistols at once, but here goes. I aim a couple shots at the Suburban's tires, but they don't connect. They don't hit the girls either, but I didn't come here to kill the other two anyway. Then all three girls are inside it and I'm standing in the headlights. The driver punches the gas as I fire both guns at the windshield.

The engine growls and tires shriek as it bears down on me. Ten feet before impact I stop firing and jump as if to land on the hood. Which I do, and then bounce up the fractured windshield and roll off the back. Everything happens so fast that I can't even process it until I'm laying in a crumpled heap on the asphalt with one pistol still in my left hand, and my whole body feeling like it's been set on fire. But fuck that.

The Suburban careens straight out onto the road, but there's no one at the wheel anymore. It jumps the median and then slams head on into a pole on the other side. I drag myself to my feet and limp one slow step at a time out into the road as sirens start to sound in the distance. A quick check of my lone remaining .380 reveals only three bullets left. The girls are making quite a commotion trying to get out of the Suburban. As the last one's feet hit the pavement I point the pistol at them from twenty feet away and all three freeze in place.

"You two," I say, gesturing to Tati and Flora with the pistol's barrel. "Listen close to what I'm about to say. Are you listening?"

All three girls nod. Mirasol looks confused to be singled out, though she ought to know better.

"My name is Mike Treadwell. Can you remember that?"

They nod again.

"Say it. Mike. Treadwell."

"Mike Treadwell," they say, their voices shaking.

"Good. Now the two of you had better run along. I want you to tell everyone you know that Mike Treadwell did this, and if you ever see him, tell Mirasol's father that now we're even for what he did to my family."

"Wh-what are you going to do to Mirasol?" Tati asks.

"The same thing I'm going to do to you if you're still standing here in ten seconds."

With that the girls are off running barefoot down the street, having lost their heels at some point in the commotion. Maybe El Frio has taken the time to explain to his daughter how fair-weather friends work. Maybe not. Maybe Mirasol understands that they couldn't have helped her anyway, because she makes no move to flee. She just stares at me with terror in her green eyes.

The sirens are getting closer. Time is running short.

"Get down on your knees," I say to Mirasol. "Now."

She does as I ask, as if it has never occurred to her that things could be any other way. Fear does that to people. It freezes them up. I've spent more hours considering what it might have done to Marie in her last moments than you would ever want to understand. I find the most comfort in believing she took it quiet, at peace, the way Mirasol seems to be taking it now.

As I point the pistol at her face she doesn't look at it, but looks into my eyes instead.

"What did my father do to your family?" she asks,

her voice almost a whisper, nothing like the passionate voice she sang in not fifteen minutes ago.

I don't know how to answer. To tell you the truth I never expected this chance to tell her about it. I aim the pistol and step forward to put the barrel against her forehead.

She leans into it, eyes still locked to my own. "You don't have to do this," she says.

The sirens are maybe a block away now. I can't explain why I'm still standing here pointing the gun at her, why she's still alive rather than a smear of brains and blood on the sidewalk.

This is not the way I imagined it at all. This is not my life. Is it? I can't get the image of Mirasol singing and dancing out of my head. Marie used to dance like that in the kitchen while she cooked. Casual, uninhibited by self-consciousness. Passionate. She was innocent. She didn't deserve to die for my mistake.

Two police cruisers screech to a stop at either end of the street. I take my eyes off of Mirasol's to see them posting up behind their car doors, pistols pointed at me. It's now or never, now or never.

One of the officers mumbles something into his cruiser's bullhorn, but I'm not looking at them now. My eyes are on Mirasol's. My mind is trying to convince my hand to pull the trigger.

"Put down your weapon," the bullhorn announces. "Now."

I put my finger on the trigger and Mirasol winces. I've got at least six red dots on my chest.

"Your father killed my wife," I say to Mirasol. "He murdered her to pay me back for losing some of his drugs. She was innocent. I came here to kill you as payback."

She starts to gasp again, then chokes it down. Her voice is full of courage as she says "I understand. Do what you need to do."

The words echo inside my head. It's now or never. I close my eyes and take a deep breath, then open them. I fire my last three shots past her head into the asphalt as a parade of bullets tear into my torso. I hit the pavement HARD. Blood is already pooling around me. My breath comes now in sobs, but I don't feel a thing anymore. Mirasol's confused face hangs above me now, still stunned from the gunfire so close to her head. I smile for the first time in years as I choke up blood that runs from the corners of my mouth. I'm ready at long last to leave this life. I've grown tired of carrying so much hatred in my heart. I guess I've never really been that man after all.

If there's a God above, I hope he will take this one decent thing into account. I pray it's not too late. Paradise is a red vinyl booth where I can sit with Ava and Marie and we can laugh and talk about everything that might have been, in another life, because none of it matters now. We'll be together again and be happy because we've learned that when everything is said and done, love is the only purpose that was ever worth pursuing. I close my eyes and picture what it will be like. I can almost feel that red vinyl bench. It's time to go home.

ABOUT THE AUTHOR

Michael Pool was born in Tyler, Texas and lives in the Dallas Fort Worth Metroplex. He is the author of the crime noir novella, *Debt Crusher*, the founder and creator of *Crime Syndicate Magazine*, and the editor for the acclaimed anthology *Fast Women and Neon Lights: Eighties-Inspired Neon Noir*. His first full-length novel, *Texas Two Step*, will be published by Down and Out Books in 2018. Find him online at
www.michaelpool.net

DEBT CRUSHER

Did you enjoy *New Alleys for Nothing Men*? If so, check out Michael Pool's hard-as-nails and sexy novella, *Debt Crusher*, out now from All Due Respect Books!

www.ingramcontent.com/pod-product-compliance
Lightning Source LLC
Chambersburg PA
CBHW071300130626
46556CB00003B/1400